NARELLE ATKINS

The Nurse's Perfect Match

D1561395

HEARTSONG
PRESENTS

Recycling programs
for this product may
not exist in your area.

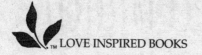 ™ LOVE INSPIRED BOOKS

ISBN-13: 978-0-373-48710-3

THE NURSE'S PERFECT MATCH

www.Harlequin.com

Printed in U.S.A.

They walked past a tall oak tree and followed the winding path, losing sight of the mansion behind them.

Fairy lights were strung in the high tree branches, twinkling in the dense foliage as if they were stars in an inky velvet sky.

Amy slowed her pace, breathing in the sweet aroma of rose and jasmine. "I wish I had my camera. The gardens are divine drenched in moonlight."

"I don't need a camera." Ben's smile widened. "I'll commit every detail about tonight to memory."

"The wedding was lovely. The bride and groom seem very happy."

He nodded. "They are a good match." He held out his arm. "Are you ready for a moonlight stroll?"

She giggled. "You sound very serious." She hooked her arm through his.

"I have serious intentions." He traced his index finger along her cheekbone. "Let's walk."

Books by Narelle Atkins

Love Inspired Heartsong Presents

Falling for the Farmer
The Nurse's Perfect Match

NARELLE ATKINS

lives in Canberra, Australia, with her husband and children. Her love of romance novels was inspired by her grandmother's extensive collection. After discovering inspirational romances, she decided to write stories of faith and romance. A regular at her local gym, she also enjoys travelling and spending time with family and friends.

But the plans of the Lord stay firm forever,
the purposes of his heart through all generations.
—*Psalms* 33:11

For my parents, Garth and Jeanette, who have always believed in me and encouraged me to follow my dreams. For my children, who provided inspiration for this story, and my husband. I love you all.

A big thank you to my amazing critique partners, Susan Diane Johnson and Stacy Monson, for your brilliant brainstorming, constructive feedback and encouraging support during the evolution and writing of this book. I thank my reader friends for their helpful comments and support: Jen B, Lisa B, Raylee B, Karinne C, Tracey H, Heather M, Merlyn S and Nicky S.

Chapter 1

The V-8 engine roared to life. Amy Wilkins stood at the side of the road, her shaky hands clutching her purse. The car sped away, dust and gravel spraying into the still night air. She pulled her jacket closer around her chilled body as the rumble of the engine receded.

Her pulse slowed and she sucked in a deep breath, glad she had chosen to wear jeans and comfortable shoes tonight. She trailed her fingertips along her arm. It stung where she had wrenched it out of his rock-solid grip. A two-mile walk home was preferable to his rotten company.

The distant glow of streetlights in Snowgum Creek and the full moon hovering overhead lit her path beside the deserted country road. She kicked a stone out of the way, not caring about the damage to her designer-label leather boot. Back home for four weeks and she'd already found trouble. If only she'd followed her mother's recommendation for a handyman instead of employing an old school friend.

Tears built in her eyes and she bit her lower lip, refusing to let them flow. She had made a mistake in trusting him, but it wouldn't happen again. Jed's charming smile had hidden a dark heart and an arrogance she didn't remember from their school days. How dare he assume she was desperate for male attention, just because she was a twenty-seven-year-old widow?

The headlights of an approaching car illuminated the isolated road. She dipped her head, hoping the driver would ignore her. The high beams blinded her and she squeezed her eyes shut. Her throat tightened as the light passed, the brakes squeaked and the vehicle slowed. *Please, Lord, keep me safe. I don't need any more problems tonight.*

Gravel crunched under the car's tires and the vehicle swung around, headlights brightening the road ahead. She sighed, her mouth set in a grim line as she turned to face it.

She stepped away from the edge of the road, a flicker of hope igniting in her heart. The people in the car could be concerned citizens who were willing to help her without asking too many questions.

The headlights dimmed and the car crawled to a stop, the passenger window lowered. A young girl rested her head on a pillow in the backseat, her innocent face serene as she slept.

Amy took a few hesitant steps forward and crouched to look inside the car. A younger boy slept beside the girl and a familiar pair of chocolate-brown eyes met her gaze from the driver's seat. Ben Morton.

She swallowed hard, captivated by the warmth emanating from his eyes. Now in his early thirties, his handsome face had matured, and the family resemblance to Luke, her boss and Ben's younger brother, was more pronounced. She hadn't spoken to Ben in years, not since she was his younger sister Rachel's best friend in high school.

His enigmatic eyes narrowed and a frown hovered over his full lips. "Amy, what are you doing out here all alone?"

She bristled at his curt tone, reminded of the times she'd gotten into mischief with Rachel in the apple orchards. "It's a long story."

She took a step back, stretching out her tense back muscles.

"Where are you headed?"

She squared her shoulders. "Home."

"Walking? At this time of night?" He leaned over and opened the passenger door.

"No, thanks. I can walk—"

"You look frozen." His voice softened. "Please get in before my kids catch a cold."

She slid into the passenger seat, warm air blasting her face from the console. He raised the automatic window and she fumbled with her seat belt, finally securing it and keeping her gaze lowered.

Silence filled the car, broken only by the idling engine and the soft breathing of the children in the back. She inhaled a hint of his aftershave, and her body tensed, aware of his muscular presence only inches away from her. Moonlight through the windshield lit up the interior of the car. How could she explain her current predicament without sounding like an idiot?

"Amy, are you okay?" His silky voice soothed her frazzled nerves.

"Yes." She unclenched her icy hands and stretched out her fingers in front of the heating vents.

"Are you sure?"

"I'm fine." She pasted a bright smile on her face, hoping he'd give up pushing for an answer.

"You don't look fine." His frown deepened. "What happened to leave you stranded out here?"

She slumped back in her seat. "It's not a big deal."

"Where's your car?"

"At home."

He raised an eyebrow. "So your car didn't break down?"

"Nope." If only his logical explanation had been the truth.

"Then how did you end up out here, miles from home?"

She twisted a long blond lock of hair around her warmed fingers. "I'd prefer not to talk about it." He'd fallen back into his big-brother role way too easily.

Ben checked the rearview mirror before steering the car back onto the road.

Amy closed her eyes for a moment, wishing she could wake up from what felt like a bad dream. This evening had turned into a nightmare, and she couldn't bring herself to tell him the full story. Heat invaded her face at the thought of Ben learning the truth.

"Which street do you live on?"

"Berkley."

"Are you near the medical clinic?"

"Around the corner. Number five." She'd fallen in love with the quaint little cottage within easy walking distance of her new nursing job.

He ran his hand through his disheveled dark brown hair. "Did someone try to hurt you?"

She nibbled her lower lip. "Not exactly."

"I can't help being concerned." He drummed his fingers on the steering wheel. "And I want to help you, if you'll let me."

"Ben, you're being very sweet, but I'm a big girl now and old enough to take care of myself."

"I can see you're all grown up—and just as stubborn as I remember."

She glanced at his profile, taking in the firm set of his mouth as they entered the outskirts of town. "I'm not stubborn. I just like doing things my way."

"Remember that time you got stuck up in the apple tree?"

She rolled her eyes. "How could I forget? It was your sister who dared me to climb that tree."

"You couldn't resist the challenge, even though it was another one of Rachel's crazy ideas."

"But I survived." She'd been thirteen, and he'd rescued her by using the cherry picker to pluck her out of the tree.

His mouth relaxed into a smile. "My Chloe is a lot like you."

"How old are your kids?"

"Chloe's nine and Declan is seven."

She sneaked a peek over her shoulder at his children. They looked cute, all snuggled up for their trip home. A journey taking longer than it should as their father took a detour back into town.

Her chest constricted. A yearning for children resurrected too many painful memories. And impossible dreams. She shoved aside the niggling guilt that accompanied thoughts of Doug, her late husband.

"Do your kids always sleep this well in the car?"

"Yes, especially after a busy day and dinner with my family."

Rachel had mentioned she helped with the care of her niece and nephew after Ben's wife had lost her battle with cancer three years ago. Amy's mother was a cancer survivor, so she understood something of what Ben had gone through with his wife's illness. But she had lost touch with Rachel for a number of years when she lived in Sydney and had only recently reconnected with her childhood friend.

"Did you see Rachel tonight?"

He nodded. "All my siblings were there until Luke was called away to the hospital halfway through dinner."

"I hope he got to eat first?"

"We'd just finished Mom's lamb roast."

"That's good." Her new boss worked crazy hours, juggling his busy medical clinic with additional responsibilities at Snowgum Creek Hospital.

He smiled. "Mom packed his dessert in a container."

"A smart idea."

"My parents are used to him rushing away during dinner."

"A downside of being a doctor."

"Yep. Chloe was disappointed that he couldn't stay. I think she'd planned to do something with him after dinner."

"That's hard." She let out a deep breath. Ben deserved to hear the truth behind why she'd been left stranded. She sat up straighter in her seat, trying to find the courage to say the right words. "I made a mistake tonight."

"We all make mistakes." He turned off the main road, heading toward her street.

"Unfortunately, I think I make more than my fair share." Her biggest mistake had been her marriage, brought to a tragic end only eighteen months earlier.

"What really happened tonight?" He stretched out his body in his seat, rolling his broad shoulders.

"I got into a disagreement that left me walking home alone."

He drove along Berkley Street. "Are you telling me someone intentionally left you in the middle of nowhere?"

"Yes," she whispered.

Ben pulled into the driveway beside Amy's cottage, keeping the engine running. A late-model hatchback sat outside her garage.

Adrenaline coursed through his body and he resisted the urge to thump the steering wheel. Who would leave someone in subzero temperatures on a dark and isolated road? Why would anyone abandon a gorgeous woman like Amy? It didn't make sense and he was determined to learn the truth.

He looked straight into her cornflower-blue eyes, holding her gaze. "You can trust me. What happened tonight?"

She leaned back in her seat, tucking pale blond hair behind her ears. Her eyes became misty and she lowered her lashes. "It doesn't matter. I handled it."

"But someone tried to do something you didn't like." Wild thoughts raced through his mind, but he reined them in, not wanting to leap to the wrong conclusions. Yet he couldn't help wondering if she needed to file a police report.

She shuddered. "I was supposed to be going to the movies in Sunny Ridge with friends."

"Did you go?"

"Yes, an old school friend drove me there."

"You didn't want to take your own car?"

"I thought about it, but my friend insisted he'd drive both of us."

He widened his eyes. Who was this guy? He held back his questions, allowing her to continue sharing her story at her own pace.

She sighed. "It's a long drive in the dark."

"Especially by yourself."

"We stopped on the way for a quick dinner. I worked out something was wrong after we arrived at the cinema."

"Were you late for the movie?"

She shook her head. "We waited as long as we could, but the other people didn't show up."

"Did you call them? Find out why they were delayed."

"No." She squirmed in her seat. "He didn't seem fazed, so we went in and watched the movie."

Ben clenched his jaw, his fears confirmed. The streetlight glowed on her beautiful face, and she turned her head toward him. He held her warm gaze, disconcerted by the sudden desire to hold her close in his arms.

Her fitted jacket and jeans accentuated how she had matured from a lanky teen into an attractive woman. She was the first woman to capture his attention since moving back to Snowgum Creek. "What happened next?"

"We drove back and he wanted to detour via his house."

Ben tightened his grip on the steering wheel, his knuckles turning white in the fluorescent light. "And you said no."

She stared at her hands, twisted together in her lap. "It got a little heated. I demanded he stop the car, and I jumped out and refused to get back in. Eventually he drove off."

He blew out a stream of air, a string of expletives on the tip of his tongue. "Who is this guy?"

"It doesn't matter. It's over and it won't happen again."

"It better not."

"I promise you, I have no plans to ever see him again." Her voice wavered and he detected a hint of anxiety behind the bravado.

"Are you sure he won't bother you again?"

She nodded. "I feel like a fool."

"No, it's not your fault he tricked you into dating him."

"But I was silly enough to believe him." She pressed her fingertips to her eyelids.

"It's okay. You're home now, and you're safe."

"Thank you. I appreciate the lift."

"You're welcome."

"I feel bad that I've taken you out of your way."

"It's not a problem. The kids have stayed asleep."

She turned around in her seat, her tender gaze lingering on his sleeping children. "They look content."

"They're good kids."

She nodded and twined her fingers through her long blond hair. "That makes your life easier."

"Yes, it helps." He drew his brows together. "Why didn't you call someone to come get you?"

"And say what? I'm the stupid girl who got conned into a date that went sour. I'd rather take the risk of walking home alone than share this embarrassing situation with anyone else."

"You're not stupid." He sucked in a deep breath. "That guy is a jerk, and if I ever get my hands on him…"

"No, Ben, it's not your problem to fix."

A part of him wished she was his problem. He had nothing to offer a sophisticated woman like Amy, and no time to even think about dating. "You take care. I'd better get my kids home to bed."

"Thanks again." She held his gaze for a moment and opened the car door. "Drive safe."

She walked up the paved path, and he waited until she had let herself into the cottage.

He rubbed his weary eyes, aware that his children should have been in bed a few hours ago. Who was the guy who had tried to hurt Amy? As soon as she was inside, he reversed down the drive and pulled out onto the street.

Ben tried to recall the names of the boys in Rachel's year at school. The ones he remembered had either married or left town. The man who'd left her may have been in a different year from Amy.

He changed gears, the clutch objecting to his hard push on the pedal. When she was younger, Amy had dated Jack Bradley, one of Luke's oldest friends. But she had married someone else and Jack had married Kate a few years ago.

Ben couldn't imagine any of Luke's or Jack's school friends doing something like this. But the guy must be from around here, someone he knew by sight. Snowgum Creek wasn't a large town.

He swung his car back onto the main road, a twenty-minute drive home ahead of him. The mystery of Amy's unsavory ex-friend plagued his mind. One day he would discover the truth.

Chapter 2

Amy finished typing up the patient notes on the computer in her clinic room. She checked her schedule and drew in a sharp breath. Ben's son was a new addition to her electronic calendar and next on her list.

Why wasn't Luke seeing his nephew? His schedule must be full again this afternoon. He was a popular doctor and, after working as a nurse at the busy medical clinic for two weeks, she understood why he'd employed her to take on some of his workload.

She glanced at the clock on the wall. Four-thirty. Her stomach lurched. Was Ben bringing in his son? Three days had passed since Ben had rescued her from the side of the road and started invading her thoughts.

She walked into the reception area. An elderly couple sat in the waiting room but her gaze homed in on Ben. His muscular back was encased in a brown fitted T-shirt as he talked to Luke outside his brother's exam room.

Declan stood beside his father, a bloodstained bandage

wrapped around his forearm. Chloe held her brother's arm, inspecting the bandage.

Luke waved in her direction. "Amy, your next patient is here."

Ben spun around, his dark eyes twinkling. "Hey, Amy, I have an injured boy for you to patch up."

She moved to Ben's side. "What happened?"

"He was playing outside with our dog and somehow caught his arm on a barbed-wire fence."

"Ouch." She turned to Declan. "I'm Amy. Let's go to my room and take a look at your arm."

"Okay." His lower lip trembled and he gripped his father's hand. "Daddy, will this hurt?"

"It won't be too bad."

"Are you sure?"

Ben brushed a couple of dark locks back off his son's forehead. "It's not like you fell out of a tree."

"Daddy, that would be silly." He stuck out his chin. "You know I'm a good tree climber."

Ben winked and glanced at Amy. "Not everyone can climb down as easily as you."

"Very funny." She narrowed her eyes, biting back a quick reply that could only embarrass her further.

Luke raised an eyebrow, shooting her a quizzical look. "I squeezed Declan into your schedule so you can clean and dress the wound."

She nodded.

"And, Ben," Luke said, "can you stick around for a few minutes after Amy takes care of Declan? I should have a gap in my schedule when you're finished."

"Sure. I'll wait for you later."

"Thanks." Luke called his next patient and disappeared into his examining room.

Amy walked ahead of Ben, smiling at Janice, their receptionist, on the way to her office. Ben and his children filed into the small room behind her.

She washed her hands and slipped on a pair of gloves. "If you can sit with Declan next to my table, I'll clean up the wound and replace the bandage."

"Sounds like a plan."

Declan wriggled closer to his father's side. He sat still and Amy removed the bandage on his arm. A small, jagged cut oozed blood.

Chloe stood beside Amy, her face lighting up. "It looks gross. Will he need lots of stitches?"

"Chloe." Ben frowned. "I'll make you wait out in the reception area if you won't stay quiet."

"But, Daddy, I'm bored." She pouted at her father, crossing her arms over her bright pink T-shirt.

Amy's lips twitched and she held back a smile. "Chloe, why don't you take a look at the books over in the corner?"

"Okay." The little girl settled on the floor rug and flicked through a book.

Amy cleaned the wound, using her soothing, professional voice to reassure Declan. "It looks worse than it really is because of all the blood. Is it stinging?"

He wrinkled his nose, squeezing his eyes shut.

"I'll be as quick as I can. Were you having fun playing with your dog when you hurt your arm?"

Declan nodded.

"What game were you playing?"

"Ball." He opened his eyes, his face relaxing into a small smile. "I chased Lily to get the ball and ran into the fence."

"That's no good. It's not fun when fences get in the way."

"Yep."

"What type of dog is she?"

Declan tapped his finger on his forehead. "Kelpie and something else I can't remember."

"That's all right. Does Lily play with you all the time?"

"Except if there's a storm."

"She doesn't like storms?"

"She's really scared of thunder and lightning."

"Okay. Are you scared of storms?"

He shook his head. "I like watching the lightning."

"You are brave, and your dad did a good job cleaning your wound."

"Actually, it was my mother who cleaned it up," Ben said. "She helps out with babysitting after school while I work in the orchards."

"She did very well. Barbed wire is nasty stuff." Amy cut a bandage to fit over the wound. "How are your parents? I've seen them in the distance at church but haven't had a chance to catch up."

"They're doing okay. Dad injured his back a few years ago and he helps out in the orchards in the morning. They bought a house in town when we moved to the farm from Sunny Ridge."

She nodded. "I'll make a point to say hello next time I see them."

"I'm sure they'd like that."

"Is Declan up-to-date with his immunizations?"

"I think so."

"Has he had a tetanus shot?"

"I can't remember. You'd better check."

"No problem. I'll look it up." She finished taping the bandage to Declan's arm. "All done. You'll be as good as new soon, and may have a tiny scar to remember this little adventure."

Declan's brown eyes, framed by long dark lashes, were identical to his father's. "Can I go play now?"

"Sure. I'll check your records with your dad."

Declan joined his sister on the floor, discovering a box of LEGO on a low shelf beside the bookcase.

Ben smiled. "I'm glad it wasn't more serious."

"Me, too." She signed onto the computer. "It'll take a couple of minutes to upload the records."

"I don't mind waiting." He leaned back in his seat, stretching out mud-splattered jeans-clad legs and work boots.

Amy cleared her throat, averting her gaze from Ben and focusing on her computer screen. "We won't need a follow-up visit unless it becomes infected."

"Okay. How are you doing?"

"Fine. The last few days at the clinic have been busy."

"Has anyone bothered you?"

She flinched. "No. I've screened my phone calls and thankfully he hasn't tried to contact me."

"Maybe he got the message you weren't interested."

"I think I made that crystal clear." The program opened and she located Declan's file. "I really don't think I'll have any more problems."

"I hope you're right. I don't mind being a witness if you need to make an official complaint."

"Thanks, but it won't be necessary." She scanned Declan's immunization history. "Declan doesn't need a tetanus shot."

"That's a relief." Ben's smile widened.

She looked at the screen, her pulse racing. "We're all done."

"Thanks, Amy. I appreciate your help."

She stood. "Please bring him back in if there's any sign of infection."

"Sure." He turned to his children. "Chloe, Declan, time to go."

The children packed up the toys and raced out into the reception area.

She smoothed out a crease near the hem of her linen shirt before following Ben to the door.

He waited in the doorway. "Have you told anyone about Saturday night?"

She shook her head. It was bad enough that he knew all the horrible and embarrassing details.

He stepped closer, concern filling his eyes. "Promise me you'll tell someone if this guy bothers you again."

"Okay." He was nearly a foot taller than she was, so she raised her chin. "But you're worrying for nothing."

"Maybe. I'd better go and check on the kids. See you later." He turned and walked away.

She closed the door and returned to her desk. One more patient at five and she was done for the day. She had time to finish writing her notes on Declan's injury and clean up before her next patient arrived. And time to think about why Ben Morton inspired thoughts and feelings she needed to shut down. He deserved a woman who was worthy of him, and she was not that person.

Ben sat in the waiting room and placed an unopened magazine on the empty chair beside him. His children had taken over the carpeted floor, playing with toy cars. He hoped Luke would finish with his patient soon.

Declan seemed happy, rolling a car along Chloe's obstacle course. It didn't look as though his arm was causing him any pain.

Ben let out a big sigh. He'd been in the far orchard when his mother had called him about Declan's injury. By the time he rode back on his tractor, she'd already dressed the wound and made an appointment with Luke at the clinic.

He smiled. The appointment with Amy had been an added bonus. Her gentle manner had put Declan at ease, and the appointment had given Ben an opportunity to check up on her. He wasn't convinced that guy would leave her alone.

Luke appeared in the waiting room, his patient now talking with Janice at the reception desk. "Ben, come on in. Janice, can you watch the kids for a few minutes?"

Janice nodded. "Your next appointment is in fifteen minutes."

Ben made sure his children were happy before following his brother into his spacious room.

"How's Declan doing?"

"Really well. Amy chatted with him while she cleaned up the wound, and he seems okay now."

"She's a great nurse."

"So I've discovered."

Luke perched on the edge of his desk, arms crossed over his chest. "You've been holding out on me."

"Huh?"

"Come on. Do you think I'm blind?"

Ben frowned. "What are you talking about?"

"I can't believe you haven't told me anything."

"I've no idea what you're on about."

Luke's eyes sparkled. "Amy. She's back in town for less than a month and you've already got something going with her."

He shook his head. "You've got it all wrong."

"I don't think so. I watched you flirt with my nurse and I caught on to your little joke about falling out of trees."

Ben placed his hands on his hips. "It's not what you think."

"You've definitely spent some time with her recently and I think it's great." Luke grinned. "It's about time you stopped mourning and started living again."

Ben ran his fingers through his dark hair. "Okay, I admit I did talk to Amy on the weekend."

"When did you see her?"

"We kind of ran into each other and ended up talking for a while."

"She's a great girl. We're friends and I've been spending a bit of time with her and Rachel."

Luke was fishing but Ben was determined not to bite. "That's good." He dropped into a seat beside Luke's desk. "I'm glad you're all friends."

Luke raised an eyebrow. "Why? Doesn't this bother you?"

Ben shook his head. He'd rather Amy spend time with his siblings than the guy who'd abandoned her.

"You know I'm happy to back off if I'm treading on your toes," Luke said.

"There's no need."

"I wonder what our sister will think about you and Amy."

Ben frowned. "Please don't say anything to Rachel about this because there's nothing to tell."

"Really?"

"We're not dating."

"Yet. I can tell you really like her and I reckon she's interested in you, too."

Ben held back a sigh. As much as he liked the idea, dating Amy or anyone else right now wasn't an option.

Luke walked around his desk and sank into his leather chair. "I'll keep my mouth shut for now. But if Rachel sees you and Amy together, I know she'll draw the same conclusion I have."

"Whatever." Once Luke got an idea in his head, it was a waste of time trying to change his mind. "Amy mentioned she went to the movies in Sunny Ridge on Saturday night."

"Did you see her at church on Sunday morning? I slept in and missed the service after filling in at the hospital the night before."

"No, I wasn't at church. Do you happen to know who she was meeting at the movies?"

Luke shook his head. "She said something about the movies on Friday but didn't mention any names. I got the impression she was catching up with old school friends she hadn't seen in years."

"That makes sense."

"Is something wrong?" Luke's eyes widened. "I get it. You're jealous and checking out the competition."

"No, it's all good, and I'm sure she has a number of admirers."

"Okay, buddy, I'll let you know if I hear of any competition, but don't wait too long before making your move." Luke chuckled. "A girl as nice as Amy won't stay single forever."

Ben glanced at his watch. "I need to take the kids home."

"Don't think this is the last time we'll be having this conversation. I know you too well."

He shrugged. Maybe talking to Luke wasn't such a smart idea. His brother was too sharp for his liking.

He refused to admit aloud that Luke was right. Amy was a beautiful woman who would draw the attention of a number of potential husbands. His stomach sank. Why did that thought sit uncomfortably in his mind?

Chapter 3

Ben diced onions on a chopping board in his kitchen. He squinted, hoping to prevent the pungent gases from irritating his eyes. If Chloe was nearby, she'd notice his watery eyes and tease him by trying to guess why her daddy was sad. And then talk about how she missed her mommy.

More than three years had passed, and he still struggled to come to terms with losing Jenny. He questioned how a loving God could take away the mother of his children.

He added the onions to the frying pan and inhaled the scent of sautéing garlic and onion. The large windows across from the kitchen island gave him an uninterrupted view of the afternoon sun disappearing beneath the horizon.

Bright hues of pink and orange filled the western sky. He never tired of watching the vibrant sunsets over his apple orchards. Or the sunrises over the Snowy Mountains to the east. His physical work outdoors had provided him with purpose as he adjusted to life as a single parent.

His sister bounced into the kitchen, a bright smile lighting up her face. "What's for dinner?"

"Spaghetti Bolognese."

"Sounds good." Rachel tucked a dark curl behind her ear and perched on a stool at the kitchen island. "I love your cooking."

He grinned. "What are the kids doing?"

"Chloe is finishing her homework and Declan is playing with his cars." She picked up a couple of sprigs of basil he'd collected from the herb garden, breathing in the fresh bouquet. "Do you want the kids showered before dinner?"

He shook his head. "I've started dinner earlier than usual. Thanks for taking care of them this afternoon."

"No problem. Babysitting in exchange for dinner works for me."

He gathered ingredients for the meat sauce from the fridge and pantry. "How has your week been?"

"Pretty busy. I have a substitute teacher taking my class for a few days next week while I do training."

"Is the training at your school?"

She nodded. "Don't worry, I can still babysit next Thursday afternoon. By the way, the cut on Declan's arm is looking a lot better."

"Yep." After two days it was healing well. He tried to ignore his disappointment over not having an excuse to schedule a follow-up appointment. Thoughts of Amy lingered in his mind.

He added ground beef to the tomato-based pasta sauce in the frying pan and filled a saucepan with water for the spaghetti.

"I wanted to talk to you about Sunday." Rachel paused, her hands resting under her chin. "I think it's time you started bringing the kids to church."

He raised an eyebrow. "Mom and Dad take them occasionally."

"Yes, but not every week. Chloe said she'd like to go more often, and Declan enjoys it, too. Don't you think maybe they need to go regularly?"

"Chloe hasn't said anything to me."

She frowned. "Do you know why?"

"No, but I'm sure you're going to tell me."

Rachel sighed. "She thinks you don't like church because you only go at Christmas and Easter."

He braced his hands on the kitchen island. "I can't fault her logic." Except it was God he had an issue with, not the church.

"Ben, please don't take this the wrong way. I should have said something earlier, but it was never the right time."

"What's wrong?"

She dropped her gaze, her voice shaky. "The last time I saw Jenny, she asked me to promise that I'd encourage your kids to go to church."

He sucked in a deep breath. Jenny had mentioned the same thing to him, but he'd forgotten all about their conversation. Until now. His memories of her were fading, and he couldn't ignore her dying wish.

"Okay, Rach, I'll take the kids to church on Sunday."

The Sunday-morning children's program at Snowgum Creek Community Church was in full swing with all the age groups in one large room. Amy worked her way around her table, helping the nine-year-old girls complete their activity sheets.

Rachel had presented a fun talk on Hannah's story to the whole group. Amy's stomach had tightened into a hard ball. She knew all too well how Hannah had suffered because she was barren.

But Hannah's story had a happy ending, and she was blessed with a son, Samuel. Despite Amy's prayers, her infertility issues remained. She bit her lip, struggling to accept her reality. Unlike Hannah, she didn't expect to be blessed with children.

"Amy, can you help me?"

Chloe's pretty face wore a big smile, warming Amy's heart. She may not be able to have children of her own, but she could be a blessing by helping these girls grow in their faith.

"Sure, Chloe. What do you need?"

"I can't find a few of the words."

Amy sat in a spare chair beside Chloe, guiding her with clues to find the elusive words in the puzzle.

A shadow fell over their table. Amy glanced over her shoulder and found Ben standing a few feet behind her, his brows drawn together.

She smiled and swiveled around in her seat. "Chloe's doing really well with her puzzle."

"So I can see." He turned to his daughter. "Are you ready to go?"

She wrinkled her nose. "No. Daddy, can I please finish my coloring first?"

He shifted his weight from one foot to the other. "Okay, sweetheart, but don't take too long."

Chloe selected a red pencil and concentrated on coloring in the picture of Hannah with baby Samuel.

Amy stood. "You can sit with her."

"No, I'm fine waiting over here." He glanced at his watch, tension radiating from his body.

"Okay." She pushed the chair under the table and moved to his side. "Do you need to be somewhere?"

"No, not really."

She looked around the table, checking to be sure her girls were settled and not needing her assistance. "Did the service finish early?"

He shook his head. "I left early."

"Was my father's sermon boring you?"

"Not at all." He rubbed his hand over his clean-shaven jaw. "He's just as entertaining as I remember."

She lifted a brow. Ben wasn't a regular at this service, yet his children seemed familiar with the kids' program.

He stood with his hands clenched by his sides, his gaze fixed on Chloe.

His discomfort aroused her curiosity. "You know," she said, "I found it hard to get back into the habit of attending church."

His eyes widened. "You took a break?"

"My late husband wasn't a big fan of church."

"Did he go to church with you at all?"

She stifled a sigh, unpleasant memories invading her mind. "He only came along with me during our first year of marriage." She'd learned too late that Doug had more important things to do on Sundays.

His shoulders relaxed and he met her gaze. "It sounds like you were in a difficult situation."

She nodded. "It wasn't easy for me to attend Sunday services when Doug made other plans." He had continually made plans that clashed with her church schedule. She had tried to compromise to keep him happy, but her faith and church attendance had suffered as a consequence.

"Jenny was very committed to the church we attended in Sunny Ridge, right up until the end."

Amy wondered if he realized how blessed he'd been to have a supportive spouse, but she just said, "When we face a crisis, it helps to belong to a caring church family."

"Yes, they were very helpful." His eyes clouded, as if he was bombarded by memories. "They brought us meals and helped me look after the kids while Jenny was in hospital."

Chloe pushed her chair back and stood. "Daddy, I'm finished now. Look at my picture."

He held her activity sheet, a smile tilting up his lips. "You've done great. Do you know where Declan is?"

Chloe tilted her head to the side. "He's probably outside playing tag or hide-and-seek with the boys."

"Can you go find him while I talk a little longer with Amy?"

"Sure, Daddy. Be back soon."

Chloe walked out of the room, passing the parents who were arriving to collect their children.

Rachel appeared at Amy's elbow. "You did well for your second week."

"Thanks. I think I'm getting the hang of it."

"I appreciate your assistance." Rachel turned to her brother. "Ben, it's great to see you here."

He nodded. "We'll be back next week."

"Excellent." Rachel's inquisitive gaze moved between Amy and Ben. "I'll leave you two to chat and I'll start packing up."

Amy stared at her now-unoccupied table, strewn with pencils and paper. "I'd better start cleaning up, too."

"Let me help." He gathered up the pencils and crayons, slipping them into the appropriate containers.

"Thanks." They cleared the table and he helped her stack the small chairs along the wall.

Chloe and Declan raced into the room, their faces flushed from running around outside.

"Hey, buddy." Ben knelt in front of his son. "Do you have your activity sheet somewhere?"

Declan's gaze darted around the room. "I'll go find it."

Chloe plopped her hands on her hips. "You lose everything."

Ben chuckled. "You can help your brother find it and then we can all go home for lunch."

Declan and Chloe dashed away, starting their search of the large room.

Ben hooked his thumb into the front pocket of his jeans,

his pale green shirt highlighting his tanned complexion. "What are your plans for today?"

She lowered her lashes, her face growing warm. Was he being polite or planning to ask her out? She swallowed hard, her throat dry and scratchy.

She clasped her moist palms together and lifted her chin. "I'm lunching with my parents and their mystery guests."

His eyes twinkled. "Wow. So your parents still do the congregation-lunch thing?"

"It only takes them around a year to lunch with the entire congregation." She grinned. "I've been tagging along the last few weeks and catching up with people I haven't seen in ages."

"An easy way to see everyone."

"Yes, and also a good opportunity to spend time with my folks."

Chloe and Declan reappeared with the missing activity sheet. The room was emptying out as everyone migrated outside for morning refreshments.

Amy swiped a few loose strands of hair off her forehead, aware that a few people, including Rachel, were paying close attention to their conversation. "I guess I'll see you all next week."

Ben nodded. "See you later."

He held Chloe's hand and walked toward the door, following Declan, who had raced ahead.

Amy took a closer look at the room. Rachel and the other helpers had done most of the cleanup while she'd been chatting with Ben.

Ben had been Amy's childhood hero. He was the big brother she'd never had who was prepared to spend time with his kid sister and her friends. She hadn't forgotten his kind heart and his willingness to rescue her from all sorts of scrapes.

The floor needed a sweep, and she headed toward the

broom closet. She inhaled the aroma of freshly brewed coffee, a smile tilting up her lips. A nice cup of coffee in the sunshine with Rachel would soothe her parched throat and hopefully stop the gossips pairing her up with Ben.

She had considered inviting Ben to stay, but he'd seemed anxious to leave. She couldn't help wondering what had driven him to leave the service ten minutes early.

"Amy, wait." Chloe reappeared in the room.

"What's up?" Amy caught a glimpse of Ben outside the room, having an animated conversation with her father.

A mischievous grin spread over Chloe's cute little face. "I left my sheet behind because I have a secret to tell you."

"Where did you put your activity sheet?" What secret did Chloe want to share?

Chloe pointed to a table beside the wall, a brightly colored piece of paper partially hidden behind a container of crayons.

Amy retrieved the activity sheet and passed it to Chloe. "That was a good hiding place."

Chloe gripped the sheet in her hand, stepping closer to Amy. "I didn't think you'd find it easily."

"You were right."

"I'm good at hiding things."

"I hope you don't hide important things from your daddy."

She shook her head. "I hide Declan's cars when he makes me cranky."

"I'm sure that just makes everything worse."

Chloe shrugged. "He does mean stuff to me. Yesterday he let Lily play with my favorite doll."

"Oh, no. Is she okay?"

"She had dog slobber all over her face and I had to wash her hair."

"Ick. That's not nice."

"I know. Do you want to hear my secret?"

"Is it a good one?"

She nodded. "It's very important you don't tell anyone."

"Okay, I promise." Amy perched on the edge of a table, lowering herself closer to Chloe's height.

"Every night I do my prayers. Auntie Rachel taught me how."

"That's great, Chloe. You know God listens to our prayers, like He listened to Hannah in our story today."

"I know." The little girl leaned in closer, her breath tickling Amy's earlobe. "I'm praying my daddy will find a new wife."

Chapter 4

Saturday-afternoon touch football was a Snowgum Creek tradition, started many years ago by Amy's father. The church-organized event now involved the wider community, and the barbecue lunch raised money for various local charities.

Amy sank into a vinyl camping chair and tilted her broad-brimmed hat back off her face. A tall gum tree on the Snowgum Creek village green provided some protection for her fair skin from the warm spring sunshine.

Rachel fussed around a fold-out table, laying out plastic plates, cutlery and salad servers. "Ben and Luke should be back soon with the meat."

"Sounds good." The aroma of sizzling beef carried in the breeze from the outdoor grills tantalized her taste buds. After a busy Saturday morning at the clinic, with no time for a break, she looked forward to a delicious lunch.

The large park in the center of town contained an open grassy area surrounded on two sides by gum trees and native shrubs. Snowgum Creek Community Church stood on the other side of the parkland. The towering stone steeple was a prominent landmark in the small town.

Rachel wiped her hands on a napkin. "I'm going to find Chloe and Declan, who seem to have disappeared again."

"Are they playing hide-and-seek?"

"Yes, hide from Auntie Rachel. After Declan's disappearing act last week…"

Amy stretched out her legs and wriggled her toes in her sneakers. "Do you think he's likely to do it again?"

"Ben doesn't think so. Chloe was given a stern talking-to about fighting with her brother and not looking out for him."

"Hopefully they'll listen."

Rachel sighed, fiddling with the hem of her T-shirt. "Kids are unpredictable, and I really appreciate you coming along today to watch the kids while we play touch footy after lunch."

"It's no trouble at all." Amy didn't have anything else planned for the afternoon. After unpacking the last box at her cottage yesterday, she embraced the opportunity to reconnect with the residents of her hometown.

"And, Rach, will I get to see you cross the line and score?"

"I hope so. I usually play on the wing and need to catch the wide passes."

"I was never any good at catching the ball." The oval-shaped leather ball, often covered in dirt and mud, used to slide through her fingers.

"Now I remember. Didn't the boys used to tease you?"

"Yep, but I ignored them and watched the game from the sideline."

"A good idea. I'll be back soon." Rachel walked away in the direction of the playground equipment.

Bright orange plastic cones were positioned in the four corners of the wide expanse of lawn. Three large gas grills, manned by volunteers from the local country fire brigade, were working overtime as hungry townsfolk stood in line.

Ben and Luke returned to the table with a platter full of sausages wrapped in bread and topped with onion. Chloe and Declan ran toward the food, their faces flushed. Rachel ambled behind them.

Amy stood and moved to the table, waiting her turn while Ben fed his hungry tribe. The kids slathered ketchup on their sausage sandwiches, grabbed their water bottles and settled in seats around the table.

Luke smiled. "Amy, what would you like?"

"It all looks good, especially the green salad."

"Ben's signature salad and the dressing is his secret recipe that he won't even share with our mother."

Frown lines appeared between Ben's eyebrows as he tried to convince his children to eat the salad.

Ben shook his head. "If only my kids agreed with their uncle."

Amy selected a sandwich and filled her plate with salad before sitting down between Ben and Luke.

She scooped a fork filled with Ben's salad into her mouth, savoring the flavors in the Asian-inspired dressing. "This is good."

He smiled. "I'm glad you like it."

Rachel slipped into a seat opposite Amy. "I eat at Ben's at least once a week, because he's the chef in the family."

"A great idea." Amy was impressed by Ben's culinary abilities.

Rachel nodded. "I sometimes wish I had Ben boarding at my house so takeaway pizza wasn't a top pick on our menu."

Luke raised an eyebrow. "If you have a medical emergency, you'll be glad I'm staying with you."

"But if I have a car emergency, which is more likely since my car is ancient, I'd rather have Ben close by."

Luke turned to Amy, his eyes twinkling. "Now you know why I feel unappreciated by my family."

She nodded, stifling a giggle. "I'm sure you'll survive."

Ben laughed. "Our sister seems to forget I come as a package deal with two kids in tow."

"Okay, Rach," Luke said. "I'll accidentally burn the cheese the next time I cook you grilled cheese on toast."

Rachel's mouth twitched into a broad smile. "You can burn the cheese without even trying."

Luke rolled his eyes but didn't respond to her gibe.

Chloe pushed her empty plate aside and turned to her father. "Can we go back to the playground?"

"As long as you're both in my sight. No hide-and-seek."

Declan nodded. "I promise."

"And you both need to stay near Amy when the game starts. I don't want a repeat of last week's fiasco."

Chloe's eyes widened and her lower lip trembled. "I promise I'll watch out for Declan and hang out with Amy."

"All right, you can both leave the table."

The children leaped out of their seats and ran back over to the playground.

Amy had listened to the banter between the siblings as she enjoyed her lunch. She caught Ben's eye and he smiled, his gaze warm.

Her heart skipped a beat and she lowered her head, focusing on her meal. Her mouth dry, she drank chilled water, gulping down the refreshing liquid. What was it about Ben's presence that sent her pulse racing?

Kara, one of Rachel's friends, approached their table. "Hey, I'm sorry to interrupt your lunch."

"No, take a seat," Rachel said. "What's up?"

"We need to talk with Luke about youth group next week. Will you both be around tomorrow?"

Luke shook his head. "I'm on call at the hospital all day. Can we talk now, before the game?"

Rachel turned to Amy and Ben. "Do you mind? Luke is hard to catch for our impromptu leaders' meetings."

"Sure. Go ahead," Ben said.

"No problem." Amy kept her tone even, not wanting Rachel or Luke to know she was intrigued by the thought of chatting alone with Ben.

Kara nodded. "We're meeting at a table near the barbecues. See you soon."

Luke and Rachel stood, cleared their plates and repacked the cooler bag with leftovers before following Kara.

Ben's gaze hovered over the playground. "How are you settling in? Do you miss Sydney?"

"Sometimes. I'll miss the beach in summer, not that I can be there long before getting sunburned."

He nodded. "I fight with my kids to get them to wear hats and sunscreen. I really appreciate you staying to watch them."

"No problem. I used to watch the game every Saturday before I moved away." Jack, her old boyfriend from her school days who loved playing touch football, was somewhere in the park with his lovely wife, Kate.

"Did you ever join in?"

She wrinkled her nose. "I'm not good at ball sports, and I only drag myself to the gym because I need to stay fit."

"Do you play other sports?"

"I used to play tennis, but these days I prefer a long walk or a swim." She had liked walking around the harbor foreshore when she'd lived on the waterfront in Sydney. The long walks were therapeutic and a good excuse to get away from the war zone at home. Doug had been sports mad, and she'd frustrated him with her reluctance to participate in all his sporting activities.

"Touch footy is the only sport I have time to play. My kids' sporting activities will soon start taking up more of my time."

"True. I'm sure all their activities keep you busy."

He nodded. "Please interrupt the game and tell me if Declan disappears again. I've spoken to him, but if Chloe stirs him up he could take off."

"We'll be fine. My plan is to hang out with them and the other kids at the playground."

"Rach blames herself for what happened but it wasn't her fault." He let out a deep breath. "She takes her auntie responsibilities very seriously."

"You're lucky to have such a great sister."

He nodded. "I don't know what I'd do without her."

"Declan's arm is healing well."

"Yes, that boy is on a mission to give me gray hair."

"He's not doing a very good job." Ben was at least four years older than she was and blessed with a full head of dark brown glossy hair. The kind of hair that tempted a woman to run her fingers through it to see if it felt as good as it looked.

His smile widened. "It's only a matter of time, now that I'm on the wrong side of thirty."

"I'm not far behind you." Her thirtieth birthday loomed ahead in a few years, and she'd never imagined she'd be widowed during her twenties.

A sharp whistle blew and Ben stood, rolling his broad shoulders. "It's time to warm up for the game."

"Good luck, and I hope your team wins."

"Thanks. See you soon." He grabbed his drink bottle and headed over to the field.

She located her sunglasses in her bag and slipped them on, ready to play with Ben's kids. Her heart constricted as the siblings swung high in the air on the swing set. Her dream of watching her own kids play in the park was never going to happen.

A week later, Ben slouched in his seat in the back row of Snowgum Creek Community Church, pondering the wisdom of his spontaneous decision to accept a lunch invitation. Before the service had commenced, Amy's parents had asked him and the children to lunch today at their home. Luke and Rachel were already going, and his sister had taken it upon herself to include him.

Would Amy be there? Because there was a possibility he might see her, he'd allowed Rachel to maneuver him into the invitation. He'd enjoyed talking with Amy last weekend and he appreciated her making the effort yesterday to watch his kids again. Despite being stuck at work until nearly two, she had come straight to the game to help him out.

He glanced at his watch, hoping the sermon would be over soon. The theme was God's unconditional love, and he struggled to relate to the concept of an all-loving God. No matter how hard he tried, he couldn't reconcile how a loving God could allow Chloe and Declan to suffer by growing up without their mother.

He was tempted to sneak out the door early to avoid the awkward interactions with well-meaning parishioners. They probably wouldn't appreciate an honest response to their unspoken questions regarding his irregular church attendance. Raw anger was entrenched in his heart, pain that was the legacy of caring for Jenny as her health deteriorated and the cancer ravaged her body.

What had his children done to deserve losing their loving and devoted mother? He was forced to accept her loss and his situation as a single parent, but righteous anger on behalf of his children still simmered in his heart and mind. He hadn't found any solace in reading the Bible as he dealt with his grief.

Chloe and Declan seemed to benefit from the children's program at church. His daughter had given him glowing reports on Amy, her favorite helper.

Music filled the sanctuary and he stood for the closing

song. He'd tuned out most of the service and had sat through it only out of a sense of obligation.

Before Jenny's diagnosis, he'd loved attending services in Sunny Ridge and worshipping with the congregation. Twinges of guilt nudged his hardened heart as he read the words of the song on the overhead screen.

What had happened to his faith? How had he ended up feeling alone and distant from God? He closed his eyes, inspired to pray for the first time in ages.

I've lost my way, and I don't know how to let go of my anger. Please forgive me and help me to raise my children in a way that would please Jenny.

He drew in a soothing breath and opened his eyes. A tiny portion of the giant burden of anger and guilt started to lift off his shoulders. Did he still believe God listened to his prayers, after so many prayers for Jenny had been left unanswered?

The service ended and he hurried toward the door, shaking hands with Amy's father before walking to the church hall to collect his children. He paused in the doorway. Chloe sat beside Amy, engrossed in conversation and pointing to something on her activity sheet.

A smile lit up his daughter's face. He could endure church for her sake and Declan's. His son sat at a different table with a group of boys, his head bent over as he colored in his activity sheet.

Amy looked up and waved, a bright smile curving her lips.

Chloe leaped to her feet. "Daddy, come look at what I'm doing."

He strolled over to his daughter's table and examined the content of her colorful sheet. "It looks great."

Chloe threw her arms around his waist. "I did it for you."

"Thanks, sweetheart." He hugged his daughter and turned to Amy. "Have you had a fun morning?"

Amy stood, her face tilted up to meet his gaze. "The girls are learning a lot and it's really encouraging to see their enthusiasm."

Chloe stepped back, her eyes brimming with mischief. "Can I please play with the other kids outside?"

"Okay."

"Daddy, you're the best." She gave him her activity sheet and followed a group of boys out the door.

Ben smiled and switched his attention back to Amy. "Are you staying for coffee?"

She lifted a brow. "Yes. Are you?"

"I have time to fill in before lunch, so I figured we may as well stay." He was looking forward to lunch, probably more than he should. There was something about Amy that intrigued him. She was fast becoming a loyal friend, and he hoped to see more of her in the future.

"Oh, you have plans for lunch?"

"It's kind of last-minute. Rachel and Luke are heading to your folks' house for lunch, and we're tagging along."

Her eyes widened. "You really are getting involved in our church again."

"It looks like it." And the way she looked at him made him glad he'd accepted the invitation to lunch.

Chapter 5

Amy dropped into a seat at the table and gathered up the spare activity sheets. Rachel had said she was coming to lunch, but had neglected to mention that Ben had also accepted an invitation.

"Rach can be pretty determined when she gets an idea in her head." Ben placed his hands on his hips. "You'll be there, won't you?"

"Yes, but I may be a little late. I told my mother I have something I need to do first." Her next-door neighbors were away for the weekend and she'd forgotten to feed their cat this morning. The cat, a cute gray tabby, should be okay, but Amy needed to find her and make sure she ate something before her owners returned that evening.

"Okay." His mouth relaxed into a smile. "Chloe will be happy to see you at lunch."

"My mother will enjoy the children's visit." Though her mother tried to hide it to spare her feelings, she knew she was disappointed she didn't have any grandchildren.

Parents started milling in the room to collect their children. Ben picked up the activity sheet Chloe had abandoned. "I'd better go and get Declan."

She smiled. "Sure. Catch you later."

He walked away and she tidied her table. By the time she'd finished cleaning up, Ben had left the hall with his kids.

Amy grabbed her purse and headed outside. The church ladies had organized refreshments outdoors to take advantage of the warmer spring weather. She joined the coffee queue, needing a pick-me-up. She'd have a quick coffee, and then she'd take off to feed the cat.

Her father joined her in the queue. "How are you doing?"

"Not bad. The kids' program went well this morning."

"Good to hear. Are you coming to lunch?"

She nodded. "After I feed the neighbors' cat. I slept in this morning and totally forgot about her."

"Have you spoken to your mother?"

"I sent her a text earlier but I haven't seen her in person." She glanced over her shoulder, scanning the crowd. "Is she here this morning?"

He nodded, lowering his voice. "Did she tell you we've invited Ben Morton and his children to lunch today?"

"No, but I saw Ben a few minutes ago and he told me."

"I thought it would be a good idea, since he's just started coming back to Sunday services." He paused. "I hear you two have become friends."

She stifled a groan. What else had her father heard? "I've been spending a fair bit of time with Rachel and Luke, and I sometimes help Ben out on Saturday afternoons by watching the kids while he plays football."

Her father nodded. "I'm glad you're settling back into life in Snowgum Creek. Your mother and I had worried you'd be bored after living in Sydney. I appreciate your help with the children's program, too."

She shuffled forward in the queue, nearly reaching the front. "I find it very satisfying to work with the younger girls. It's been good for me for a number of reasons."

"I agree." He poured coffee into two mugs. "We need to touch base more often."

"I know. Work has been busy, but I'll be in touch if I have some spare time this week. Mom said she wanted me to try and come around for dinner at least once a week." She added milk and sugar to her coffee mug.

Her father smiled. "Sounds like a good plan. We miss you, and it's so good to have one of my girls living close by again. I'll see you at lunch."

"Yes." She stirred her coffee and searched the outdoor terrace area for Rachel.

Rachel was talking with Kara in the distance near the kids' play area. Amy turned around to find Ben standing beside her.

He grinned. "There are a lot of people here today."

She met his warm gaze, inhaling the distinctive scent of his aftershave. He looked good, dressed in a casual shirt and jeans. "I think this group is larger than normal. The spring weather must be encouraging everyone to stay."

The sky was an intense azure, with a couple of white puffy clouds floating in the gentle breeze.

She sipped her coffee. "Do you know most of the people here?"

"There are only a few unfamiliar faces, and everyone has been friendly."

"I need to take off as soon as I finish my coffee."

"Why? I mean, do you have plans before lunch?"

His question hung in the air between them. There was nothing else to do but confess the truth.

She nibbled her lower lip. "I have failed in my good-neighbor duties."

"How?"

"I forgot to feed my next-door neighbors' cat this morning. She's an outdoor cat and all her food is stored in the laundry room."

Chloe appeared at her father's side and grabbed hold of his hand.

"I need to find the cat and feed her as soon as possible."

Chloe's eyes lit up. "Amy, do you have a cat?"

She shook her head. "I'm looking after my neighbors' cat and I need to feed her before lunch."

"I love cats. Can I help you?"

"It's your father's call, and the cat may be cranky because she missed her breakfast."

"Daddy, please." Chloe turned pleading eyes to her father.

He glanced at his watch. "We do have time to swing by your place on the way to lunch. That is, if you'd like two little helpers?"

"Sure." She swallowed her last mouthful of coffee. "I'm leaving now. Do you remember the address?"

He nodded. "I'll find Declan and we'll meet you outside your house."

"Sounds good. Or, if I beat you there, let yourself into the backyard through the neighbors' gate next to my garage."

"No problem. See you soon." He held Chloe's hand and wove through the groups of people toward the kids' play area.

She returned her coffee mug to the kitchen and made her way to her car, thankful she'd driven to church today.

Minutes later she parked in her driveway and ducked around the front fence and into her neighbors' yard. Unlocking the side gate, she looked around, hoping to find Mischief somewhere nearby.

She frowned. "Mischief, time for breakfast. Where are you, Mischief?"

The bushes along the side fence rustled, and the tabby

cat gave her a long look before ambling toward the external laundry door, located at the back of the house.

The side gate squeaked open. Chloe and Declan appeared, followed by Ben.

Chloe smiled. "She's a cute cat. What's her name?"

"Mischief."

"Can I pat her?"

"Not yet." She found the laundry key and opened the door. "Let me feed her first and then she may be happy to have some attention."

Mischief let out a loud meow before stalking into the laundry. Her string of meows made her displeasure at being kept waiting known to everyone.

Ben chuckled, standing back in the entrance to the laundry. "You are in trouble."

"I know. I'm thankful she was close by. She may forgive me one day."

Chloe sneaked under her father's arm, a hopeful look in her eyes. "Can I come inside and help you?"

"Sure." She located a tin of food and a bag of dry cat kibble. "If you can, please scoop some dry food into one side of her dish. I'll put the tinned food in the other."

Amy opened a small bar fridge, found a carton of milk and poured some into a separate bowl.

Mischief meowed and rubbed her sleek body against Amy's legs, her tail curling around her calves.

Chloe served the dry food and placed the bowl on the tile floor.

Mischief let out another appreciative meow before scarfing down half of it. Amy added the pungent canned fish. The cat alternated between the food and milk, sating her appetite.

Declan hung back, tapping his finger on his lips. "Why is Mischief having her breakfast now?"

"Long story, but she can now sleep the day away with a full stomach."

Mischief licked the food bowl clean and drank all the milk. Amy topped up her water bowl outside the laundry door.

Ben smiled. "You have a contented cat."

Amy nodded, crouching to hold Mischief now that she'd finished her meal. Chloe and Declan took turns patting the cat, who purred in response to their attention.

Ben crossed his arms over his chest, leaning against the doorframe. "Do you have a cat?"

She shook her head.

"We have wild cats that hang around the orchards." Chloe frowned. "But they're no fun because they run away if you go anywhere near them. Lily is our pet dog."

"That's right. I remember you and Declan talking about Lily at the clinic."

"She's a friendly dog and she really likes licking people."

"She sounds like a lovely dog." Amy had wanted to get a dog in Sydney when she'd lived in a big house with sprawling grounds. But Doug had refused, claiming they were too much work and an inconvenience he didn't need.

She stood, allowing the cat to rush outdoors to her cozy spot in the bushes.

Chloe pursed her lips. "Where did she go?"

Her father placed his hand on her shoulder. "Back to a place where she won't be bothered by children. We'd better get going or we'll be late for lunch."

The children cleaned up with Amy before everyone returned to their vehicles.

Ben unlocked his car and his kids piled inside. "Would you like a lift?"

She shook her head. "I may stay later, depending on what my mother has planned. Dad has already spoken to me today about how much he misses me and wants us to spend more time together."

"Fair enough." He opened his car door. "See you there."

The kids settled in their seats and her heart tugged. Ben's children were adorable and creeping their way into her affections. Her yearning for children intensified and she bit her lip, raw emotion choking her throat.

Lord, why didn't You bless me with children? It's bittersweet hanging out with Chloe and Declan when having a family of my own is impossible.

Ben arrived at Amy's parents' home with five minutes to spare. Luke's Jeep was parked out the front and he assumed Rachel had caught a lift with their brother.

He knocked with the heavy brass knocker. Amy's mother opened the door. A petite blonde, she looked like an older version of her daughter.

"Please come in." She stepped back. "Luke and Rachel are in the family room."

"Thanks." The children ran ahead and Ben strolled through the modern home to an open-plan kitchen adjoining a dining area. A spacious family room lay ahead through a wide doorway. Luke and Rachel sat on a sofa opposite Amy's father.

Amy's mother paused in the kitchen. "Would you like a drink?"

"Yes, please. Whatever you have going."

"Juice, water, soda. What would the children like?"

"Water is fine for all of us, thanks."

"Okay." She organized a tray with a water jug and three cups. "I'll bring this through to the family room."

"No, let me," he said. "You look busy. Do you need any help?"

She shook her head. "I only have a couple of things left to do." She passed over the tray. "You go ahead, and lunch will be ready soon."

"Sounds good." He greeted Amy's father and his siblings before pouring drinks for his children. He relaxed into a comfortable recliner opposite a wide-screen television.

Luke sipped his soda. "Where have you been? You left church quite early and we wondered if you'd gotten lost."

The phone rang and Amy's father rose. "I'd better answer that. Please excuse me." He rushed away toward the kitchen.

Chloe perched on the sofa between her uncle and aunt. "We helped Amy feed Mischief."

"Mischief." Luke raised an eyebrow. "I didn't know Amy had a new pet."

"No, silly," Chloe said. "It's her neighbors' cat, a tabby that let me feed her cat food and pat her."

"Okay." Luke shot Ben a quizzical look. "So, Ben, did you enjoy your cat-feeding detour?"

Rachel coughed, nearly choking on her mouthful of water.

Ben frowned. "Rach, are you okay?"

She nodded, clearing her throat. "I thought you hated cats?"

He shrugged. "Chloe wanted to meet the cat and we had the spare time."

Luke narrowed his eyes. "I'm sure you did."

Light footsteps sounded on the wooden floorboards and Amy appeared. "I'm sorry I'm late."

"No, you're fine," her father said, entering the room behind her. "Lunch will be ready very soon."

"Does Mom need any help?"

Her father shook his head. "We've set the outdoor table because it's a gorgeous day."

Chloe followed Declan to a piano situated in the far corner of the room. She opened the lid and tested a couple of keys.

"Chloe." Ben stood. "Have you asked permission to touch the piano?"

Her lower lip trembled. "I'm sorry. Am I allowed to use it?"

Amy's mother joined the children by the piano. "Of course you can. These days Amy is the only one who plays it, and she rarely uses it when she visits."

Amy smiled. "Chloe, do you know how to play the piano?"

She shook her head. "I'd like to learn. My mommy was a really good piano player. I remember her playing nursery rhymes and singing to us."

Ben sucked in a deep breath, long-forgotten memories filling his mind. He was glad Chloe still had vivid memories of her mother, even though she was only five when Jenny passed away.

He wandered over to the piano. Chloe sat on the long piano bench seat beside Amy.

Chloe looked at Amy, wide-eyed and with a hopeful expression on her face. "Can you play something?"

"Okay, although I may be a little rusty. I use a keyboard at home."

Ben leaned against a wall and listened to Amy play a classical piece he recognized but couldn't name. Her long, slender fingers flew over the keys, and the sweet, melodic sound tantalized his senses. Her timing and touch were beautiful, and her face relaxed as her fingers glided over the ivory keys.

He closed his eyes, transported back to a time when Jenny's love of music had filled his home with happy tunes. He missed her, and he allowed the cathartic music to wash over him.

The song ended and he opened his eyes. Amy was a talented pianist.

Everyone clapped and he added his applause.

Luke stood beside the piano. "Amy, that was exquisite. Why aren't you playing music in church?"

"I'd rather focus my energies on the kids' program."

"Daddy." Chloe reached for his hand. "Can I please have piano lessons so I can learn to play like Amy and Mommy?"

His heart squeezed tight in his chest. Even if he knew a good piano teacher, he couldn't afford the cost of piano tuition. "I don't know, sweetheart. We'd have to find a piano teacher who could visit us, and I'd need to take a look at my budget first."

Rachel's eyes widened and she clapped her hands together. "Amy, if I remember correctly, aren't you a qualified piano teacher?"

Amy paused, examining her fingernails. "Yes, but I haven't taught for quite a few years."

"That's right," Rachel said. "I remember you used to teach piano when you were working at the bank."

He raised an eyebrow. "That's a while ago. Did you teach piano in Sydney?"

She shook her head. "I was too busy completing my nursing studies to teach."

Chloe turned to Amy. "Would you be my piano teacher?"

"Chloe." Ben's tone was sharp and he squared his shoulders. "That is not your decision to make."

His daughter's lower lip trembled. "Daddy, I'm sorry, but I really want to learn."

Luke placed a firm hand on Ben's shoulder, his voice low. "I can help you pay for some of the lessons if Amy is available to teach."

He stifled a groan. The last thing he wanted was to look like a charity case, but he turned to his brother, seeing his offer as a genuine attempt to help his niece. "Thanks."

"No big deal."

He met Amy's gaze. "Are you interested? You'd need to come out to the farm, and I'll pay you the going rate, taking into account your travel expenses."

She lifted a brow. "Last week when I was unpacking I

found the box with all my teaching materials. If Chloe is keen…"

"Yes, please, Amy. I really want to learn."

Ben let out a deep breath, remembering how Jenny had wanted her children to learn piano. "Okay, we can work out the details later."

"Thanks, Daddy. You're the best." His daughter embraced him in an enormous hug and an intense love flowed into his body. How could he say no to his precious daughter?

He met Amy's gaze. "It looks like we have a deal."

Amy smiled. "You may have to be patient with me."

"I'm sure you'll do great." He let go of his daughter, a new lightness pouring into his heart. It would be good for Chloe to explore one of her mother's passions, and he couldn't deny he'd look forward to Amy visiting his home.

Chapter 6

Amy drove along a narrow country road, thankful there weren't any cars coming the other way as she dodged potholes. Ben's farm was the next turn after the rise of the hill.

She had finished work at lunchtime to compensate for the additional hours she'd spent at the clinic on Saturday. Her sheet music and tuition books were packed in her bag on the passenger seat. She hoped she'd remember how to teach a brand-new piano student. Her heart warmed at the pleasure and excitement Chloe had shown when Ben had made arrangements for her to teach Chloe every Wednesday after school.

She turned onto the dirt track leading to the farm entrance. Rows of apple trees covered the sloping hills that surrounded the house. A wraparound veranda circled the brick home, and a cottage garden bloomed outside the front entrance.

She drove around to the back of the house. Ben waved and jumped off a tractor near one of the sheds. She parked under a tree and walked over to the shed. Ben and Declan were investigating various pieces of machinery.

"Hey, Amy." A broad smile covered Ben's tanned face. "What are you two up to?"

Declan lifted a chunk of metal. "We're fixing an old tractor."

"Sounds fun. Where's Chloe?"

Ben nodded. "She should be inside finishing her homework."

"Okay, I'll head over to the house."

Strips of pink highlighted the western sky, the sun sitting low on the horizon. She'd be driving home in the dark after their half-hour lesson.

Ben wiped his grease-covered hands on a clean rag. "Would you like tea or coffee?"

"No, I'm fine, thanks. I picked up a latte in town to drink on the way, and I don't want to interrupt what you're doing."

"Sure, but we're nearly finished. Declan has reading to do for homework before dinner."

Declan wrinkled his nose. "I don't like reading, and the stories are boring."

His father placed a firm hand on his shoulder. "That's because you keep reading the same stories. With more practice, you'll move up a level and have a choice of different stories."

"Do I have to read tonight?"

"Yes, you can read while Chloe is occupied with her piano lesson."

She gave Declan a reassuring smile. "I'm sure the stories will get more interesting soon. I'll see you both later."

She turned on her heel and walked along a pebbled path to the back door. A range of vegetables grew in the well-kept gardens.

She knocked on the closed screen door. "Chloe, are you there?"

"Yes." Footsteps sounded as Chloe ran through the house and appeared in the doorway. "I'm so happy it's Wednesday, and I've been looking forward to my piano lesson all week."

"I'm glad to hear that." She followed Chloe through the house to the sitting room at the front. A baby grand piano was the centerpiece of the room. A sofa and coffee table were positioned to overlook the wide windows and front garden. Amy found the room warm and inviting.

Chloe opened the piano lid and played a couple of notes. She was thankful the instrument sounded in tune.

"Does anyone play your piano?"

She shook her head. "Not since Mommy went to heaven."

"Okay, then, let's get started." Amy was glad Chloe's enthusiasm wasn't dimmed by thoughts of her mother. It must be hard to lose a parent at such a young age. Rachel had mentioned that Chloe's mother had been an excellent pianist and had spent a lot of time practicing.

Amy hoped she could encourage Chloe's passion for music and help her mother's legacy live on, plus foster any musical talent Chloe had inherited from her.

Ben and Declan cleaned up before moving through the house to the kitchen.

"Daddy, I'm hungry."

"Dinner won't be long."

He pulled a face. "I'm really, really hungry."

"Here's an apple." He rinsed a juicy red apple from his orchard.

"I'm sick of apples."

"Well, it's either an apple or you can wait for dinner. Your choice."

"Okay, I'll have the apple." Declan bit into the succulent fruit, a tiny bit of juice dribbling down his chin. "Can I watch TV?"

"Not until you've done your reading."

Ben sat with Declan at the table in the dining area adjacent to the kitchen. He helped his son work through the book, pleased that Declan was sounding out new words and making an effort to improve his reading.

Ben signed the homework reading sheet. "You can watch TV in the family room until dinner."

"Thanks, Daddy." Declan scooted away from the table and headed into the family room.

Ben selected a variety of fresh vegetables from the fridge and pulled out a chopping board, ready to prepare the ingredients for a stir-fry. He grew a variety of produce and saved a lot of money at the grocery store. The chicken was sliced up in the fridge, ready to be added to the wok.

He placed water and rice in the electric rice cooker, switching it on. He glanced at his watch. Chloe's lesson was due to end in around ten minutes.

Curious, he opened the French doors leading from the dining area to the front of the house and closed the door to the family room, where Declan watched a cartoon.

Gentle piano tones drifted down the hall from the sitting room. Chloe was learning scales, and he listened to the repetitive note pattern, thankful that Amy had agreed to teach his daughter.

He resisted the temptation to sneak up the hall and stand outside the sitting room. It was good for Chloe to be independent, and he could hear Amy's melodic voice as she gently spoke with his daughter.

He returned to the kitchen and finished chopping up the stir-fry vegetables. He'd throw together the dinner after Amy went home.

The music lesson ended, and Chloe tore down the hallway, a massive smile on her face. "That was so much fun. Did you hear me?"

"Yes." He met Amy's gaze over the top of Chloe's head.

"You sounded great. Do you have something to practice for next week?"

"Amy has given me a folder with music and instructions on what to do." She glanced around the room. "Where's Declan?"

"Watching a cartoon."

"Cool. I want to watch TV. Amy, see you later."

Amy smiled. "Don't forget to practice."

"I won't." Chloe ran toward the family room to join her brother.

Ben scraped the last of the stir-fry ingredients off the chopping board and into a bowl. "The lesson seemed to go well."

She leaned back against the kitchen island. "Chloe is keen to learn and picks things up quickly."

He nodded. "I'm happy she was cooperative and well behaved."

"She's a pleasure to teach." She paused. "You've done a great job with your kids."

"I do my best." It was hard being a sole parent, and he was glad his parents and siblings were involved in his children's lives. "Are you going to start doing more piano teaching?"

She shrugged. "With my full-time nursing job at the clinic, I don't have a lot of spare time. Occasionally I fill in at the hospital when they're short staffed."

"Do you work nights?"

"Yes, sometimes Saturday night. Sunday is my only day off, and I'm committed to the kids' program on Sunday mornings."

"I assume you attend the evening service, as well."

"I usually go with Rachel and occasionally Luke, depending on his schedule. The youth group is growing, which is encouraging."

He nodded. It wouldn't be long before Chloe was old enough to attend youth group. "Kids seem to grow up fast."

"True. Is the same time next week okay with you?"

"Yes, as long as you don't mind driving back in the dark."

"I'll take it easy and watch out for kangaroos." She stood straighter, clasping her hands together. "I should go. I don't want to be responsible for delaying your dinner."

"Would you like a drink, tea or coffee, before you leave?"

She shook her head. "I'm going to buy a coffee with dinner on the way home."

"What are you having?"

"Not sure. Maybe pizza or Chinese. Or fish and chips. I'll think about what I feel like during the drive."

"Do you cook?"

"Not as much as I used to. I like to cook, but it's not as much fun for just one person. When I do cook, I usually make extra to freeze so I don't have to cook every day. Now I need to get into the habit of eating once a week at Mom and Dad's. I'll have to cook even less."

She walked to the table and fished her keys out of her purse.

"I'll walk you out and turn on the outside lights." He must remember to keep the lights on each Wednesday evening.

They headed out the back door, and Ben switched on the lights, flooding the backyard.

"Thanks." She walked to her car and beeped open the locks.

"Next week I'll have a check ready to cover the lessons for the remainder of the school term."

"Sure, but there's no rush."

He nodded. Luke had contributed some money toward Chloe's lessons. He appreciated his brother's kindness and generosity. Ben's living-expenses budget was tight for at least the next six months. He needed a bumper crop, combined with good apple prices, to try to get ahead financially next year.

She stowed her bag on the passenger seat and met his gaze. "See you later."

"'Bye." He smiled as she drove along the well-worn track to the road, her headlights disappearing into the inky night. He couldn't help being drawn to her warm and generous nature.

If only his circumstances were different. He'd become accustomed to the loneliness of being single, although now that his children were older and staying up later, the long evenings by himself were becoming shorter. He had nothing financially to offer Amy or any other woman. He couldn't even afford to fully cover the cost of piano tuition.

He walked back to the house, running his hand through his hair. Amy deserved someone who had more time and money to spend on her. Someone she could marry and start a family of her own with.

Despite his attraction, he wasn't good enough for her and he couldn't give her what she needed. They couldn't have a future together and it was pointless dwelling on something that was futile. She was a friend, and he had to remind himself that this was all he could expect and more than he deserved. If only his thoughts didn't turn in her direction so often.

Amy finished updating her patient files in the computer at the clinic. A steady flow of patients had kept her busy. She glanced at the time on her phone. It was after eleven-thirty and she hadn't stopped for her morning coffee.

She stood and slipped her purse over her shoulder. She had time to buy a latte from a café up the road before her next patient was due. One day she hoped to convince Luke to invest in a coffee machine for their staff kitchen. Living in Sydney had spoiled her, regarding her tastes in coffee.

She closed the door to her room and walked through the reception area. Ben stepped toward her, the only person in the waiting room.

"Hey, Amy, do you have a minute?"

Her heart skipped a beat. "Do you have an appointment with Luke?"

He shook his head. "I was in town and thought I'd stop by to ask a question."

"Okay. I'm just heading out to buy a latte." She paused. "You can come with me and talk on the way."

"Thanks." He fell into step beside her and they walked along the path to the street.

"What's up?"

"I have a favor to ask."

She lifted a brow. "Do you need a babysitter?"

"No, my family has that covered." He smiled. "It relates to our conversation a few weeks ago after Amy's piano lesson when you mentioned you like cooking."

She nodded. "What do you need?"

"Rachel mentioned that you're coming to our parents' anniversary party this weekend."

"Yes, it was lovely of them to invite me."

"I was wondering if you could help me out in the kitchen. I know it's an imposition, but I looked at the menu Luke and Rachel proposed and worked out that I need another pair of hands. My sister can help, but I'd prefer to free up her time to look after the guests. We're expecting fifty."

"Wow." She stopped at the curb, waiting for a truck to pass by before heading across the road to the café.

"Yes, I only learned about the numbers last night. I thought they had invited thirty guests, but my parents must have added people to the list after the invites were sent."

They crossed the road and strolled into the café. Two

customers waited in front of the counter and Amy stood behind them.

"What do you think?" Ben placed his hands on his hips, his eyes sparkling.

"I'll have to go to church and do the kids' program first, which means I won't be able to help you on Sunday morning."

"That's okay. I'll skip church and get Rachel or my parents to take the kids in the morning."

"A good idea."

He grinned. "I'll get a lot done without the kids under my feet."

"True. I can take off straight after the kids' program is finished." She shuffled forward in the queue, tilting her head to the side. "What's on the menu?"

"Barbecued meat with salads, which is good. We can make the salads in advance. The problem is that the desserts have a few last-minute fiddly things to organize. Pavlova, cheesecake and chocolate mousse. Plus ice cream for the kids."

"Okay, it sounds manageable." She drew her brows together. "Will you have enough fridge space?"

"Just. A number of guests are bringing salads, and I'm doing all the desserts. The large number of people will make it very busy."

"Maybe you should have hired caterers?"

He grinned. "Had I known we'd have fifty guests, I definitely would have looked into other options."

She moved to the head of the line. "Can I get you something?"

He shook his head. "I'm good."

She ordered and paid for her latte, then moved to the side while the barista made her coffee.

"It should be fun, but are you sure you don't want any help with making the desserts?"

"It's fine. I can make everything the day before. Your help in my kitchen on the day is all I need. Luke and Rachel are coming over on Saturday to help get the house ready. We'll eat outside on the veranda and Jack has volunteered to help Luke man the grill."

"It sounds like you have everything organized."

"Oh, we won't be at touch footy on Saturday, either."

"That works well for me. The hospital asked if I could do a late Saturday-afternoon shift. They only called this morning and I was going to let you know that I'll need to work."

He nodded. "No problem, and please don't ever say no to work so you can watch my kids."

"It's more fun to hang out with your kids." Her name was called out and she collected her coffee from the counter.

He opened the café door. "I'd better be going. I still have a lot of work to get done on the farm today."

"Sure." She walked into the bright sunshine. They crossed the road and within minutes reached Ben's truck.

She sipped her latte, inhaling the aromatic coffee blend. Bliss. She loved a good coffee.

His eyes softened. "I'll see you tomorrow afternoon for Chloe's lesson."

"Yes, I'm looking forward to it. And please let me know if there's anything else I can do for the party."

"Sure, and thanks again. I appreciate knowing I'll have your help."

"Too easy. See you later." She headed up the path to the clinic, her step light. Why did spending time with Ben put a big smile on her face?

Chapter 7

Amy drove along the dirt track toward Ben's farm. She glanced at the clock on her dashboard. Ten in the morning. She'd made good time.

Rachel had found a replacement for Amy at church this morning. Luke and Jack were coming over at eleven to look after the grill. The guests were due to arrive at midday, and Ben planned to serve lunch at one.

The cloudless sky was a good sign that the weather would provide another gorgeous spring day. Rain had been scarce, which didn't bode well for the summer.

Amy parked under a gum tree near the shed at the back of the rambling homestead. She grabbed her purse and shopping bag containing fresh cream and fruit for the topping on the pavlova meringue dessert and the fruit platter. The melons weighed down the bag as she walked to the back door.

She knocked on the open door. "Ben, I'm here."

"Come in," he called out.

She headed along the hall and into the kitchen. Ben stood at the kitchen sink, rinsing lettuce for a salad. His hair was disheveled and he wore an old T-shirt and jeans.

"Hey." He smiled, his eyes twinkling. "Thanks for coming by early."

"No problem. Now, what can I do?"

He glanced at her shopping bag. "There's space in the fridge for the cream and fruit. Jack is storing all the meat in his fridge and will bring it over in cooler bags so it won't take up fridge space."

"I'll unpack everything now. I can make the fruit platter just before lunch so it won't need to go in the fridge."

"Good idea. We'll whip the cream at the last minute, as well."

She opened the fridge, her gaze homing in on an enormous glass bowl of chocolate mousse and a large baked cheesecake. "The desserts look great. You've been busy."

He nodded, spinning lettuce to remove the excess water. "I'll be glad when it's over. Chloe is complaining we have no food in the fridge that she is allowed to eat."

She smiled. "There may be leftovers, if she's lucky."

He opened a drawer and handed her an apron. "Use this to protect your clothes."

"Thanks. I forgot to bring one. I'm not used to cooking in party clothes."

His smile widened. "You look good. I like your hair up."

Warmth flooded her face. "I pulled it back off my face for hygiene reasons."

"It looks nice." He chopped a range of salad vegetables, adding them to a large crystal bowl.

"Is this your signature salad?"

He nodded.

"Does this mean I can learn how you make your famous dressing?"

"As long as you keep it a secret." He grinned. "And

don't make it yourself and serve it to my family. I've enjoyed tormenting Luke for years by not telling him the ingredient list."

She giggled. "He's not happy about it, is he?"

"He'll cope, not that he'd ever make it himself. Cooking isn't his strong suit."

She perched on a stool at the kitchen island, her back facing Ben as she sliced a couple of long French bread sticks.

Before long, Luke and Jack arrived. After stopping in the doorway to say a brief hello, they headed outside to set up the grill.

Luke wandered back into the kitchen, searching for utensils to use on the grill. He eyed the salad Ben had covered in plastic wrap. "Amy, did you see the ingredients he used in the dressing?"

She shook her head. "I've been busy slicing up bread sticks."

Ben shrugged his shoulders. "Not everyone cares to know the recipe."

His brother narrowed his eyes. "Amy, are you sure you didn't see anything?"

She wiped her hands on the front of her crisp white apron. "I've been busy. Look at all the bread I've sliced."

Ben placed the salad in the fridge. "I might tell you one day."

"I doubt it. The grill is ready." Luke located a spare chopping board and knife. "We have half an hour until the guests arrive. Rachel and our parents should be here with the kids any minute."

"Okay." Ben let out a deep breath. "Amy, I'm going to have a quick shower and get ready. Why don't you sit down and take a break? You've been working nonstop for the last hour."

She lifted a brow. "Are you sure there's nothing else that needs to be done now?"

He nodded. "Rest up before we start on the desserts. Make a tea or coffee. Luke, do you or Jack want anything?"

Luke shook his head. "We're good."

"And, Luke, can you please put aside some meat for us?"

"You're not eating outside with everyone else?"

Ben shook his head. "I don't think we'll have time, since Mom and Dad want dessert served at two and the anniversary cake at three."

"You can't hide away in the kitchen." He raised an eyebrow, a teasing lilt entering his voice. "Or are you planning your own private lunch with Amy?"

She sucked in a deep breath, dropping her gaze. Did her willingness to help Ben make it look as if they were dating?

"Our work in the kitchen is done once dessert is served." Ben held his brother's gaze. "Rachel and Kara will focus on the cleaning up and I'll tackle the remaining dishes after everyone has left."

"Fair enough. I think everything should run like clockwork."

He nodded. "When is Caleb arriving?"

Luke frowned. "He said he'd be here by twelve, but you know what our little brother is like."

Amy was glad the conversation had moved safely away from her relationship with Ben. "What is Caleb up to these days? I haven't seen him in years, since he was a kid."

Ben met her gaze. "He's a real-estate agent in Sunny Ridge."

"And his job takes more of his time than mine does," Luke said.

She widened her eyes. "Is that even possible?"

"Yep." Ben smiled. "I really want to see Caleb today. It has been way too long since his last visit, and I haven't had a chance to visit him in Sunny Ridge."

Luke sighed. "Yes, he has certainly worked out how to avoid doing any work for our family get-togethers. I'd better go outside." He lifted a bag of onions. "These won't chop themselves."

She wrinkled her nose. "You did get the short straw."

He nodded. "My sunglasses will protect my eyes from the worst of the fumes."

"Why don't you chop them up here?" She indicated the clear bench space beside the double sink. "They'll sting your eyes less if you soak them in cold water first."

"Okay." He adjusted his designer-label sunglasses on top of his head.

Ben smiled. "I'll be back soon."

She nodded and watched him saunter out of the kitchen.

Luke set up his chopping board beside the kitchen sink. "You might want to keep your distance."

"No problem." She switched on the electric kettle. "Tea or coffee?"

He shook his head, slipping his sunglasses over his eyes before he started peeling and slicing the onions.

"You know you could have bought presliced onions?"

"Yes, but I wasn't able to shop until late yesterday and they'd sold out."

She poured her tea and added milk, jiggling the tea bag in the ceramic cup.

"No coffee for you?" he asked.

"Ben only has instant, and it's not as good as the instant at work." She frowned. "Which isn't particularly good, but at least it's drinkable."

"Ouch." Luke pretended to flinch. "You're not going to let up until I buy the expensive machine."

She shrugged. "I'm investing in the local economy by purchasing at least one latte per day."

"You seem to know your way around Ben's kitchen."

"I'm here every Wednesday afternoon."

"And my brother doesn't look after you by making you tea?"

"He's usually occupied with Declan."

Luke scraped a pile of onions into a stainless-steel bowl. "I'm half-done."

"Do you want me to take over?"

"No, I'll struggle on. By the way, you are much esteemed."

She lifted a brow. "In what way?"

"To be allowed in Ben's kitchen while he's making his salad."

She laughed. "His powers of diversion are masterful. That dressing was made before I even knew he'd started."

"No, seriously. He doesn't like me or Rachel in the kitchen. Now, me, I can understand, but Rachel is a pretty good cook when she puts in the effort."

She sipped her tea. "I didn't realize this."

"I think my brother really likes you."

Her face flushed and she stared into her teacup. "I don't think so. We're just friends."

"Yes, but it's possible it could become something more if that's what you want. My brother hasn't shown any real interest in a woman since Jenny died, until you came along."

"Luke, this conversation is a little awkward because you're my employer."

"We're also friends. Look, I just wanted you to know that I'd be happy for both of you if something did happen. You'd have my support."

She smiled. "Thanks, but I think you've got it all wrong."

He scraped the last of the sliced onions into the bowl. "Maybe, but time will tell."

She gulped down the remainder of her tea. She liked hanging out with Ben, and she couldn't deny he was an attractive man who sent her pulse racing. But she couldn't give him what he needed. She'd been a failure as a wife the first time around. Ben and his children deserved someone better.

* * *

Ben ran his fingers through his hair, slick after his brief shower. At least he'd remembered to iron a shirt last night. The house was quiet as he wandered back along the hall to the kitchen. His parents should be here soon with his children.

He paused near the entrance to the kitchen. Amy sat on a stool at the kitchen island, slicing fruit for two large platters. A pile of melon and other fruit peelings was stacked on a dinner plate beside her chopping board.

She wore an elegant shirt and long skirt that looked designer label. All her clothes were good quality and he guessed she was financially well-off.

She swiveled around in her seat, her beautiful smile lighting up her face. "I thought I'd make a start on the fruit."

"Good idea. Have you seen my parents?"

She shook her head. "Rachel arrived a few minutes ago. She mentioned your folks were ducking home first."

"Okay." His apron was slung over a chair in the dining area. She'd tidied up for him, and he'd need the apron later because he owned only a couple of decent shirts.

Chloe's and Declan's footsteps sounded in the hall.

"Daddy, where are you?" Chloe called out.

"In the kitchen."

She raced into the room and threw herself at him, wrapping her arms around his waist. "I missed you."

"I missed you, too." He lowered his head and dropped a kiss on her forehead, breathing in the light floral scent of her shampoo. "You need to hurry and get dressed. Your party dress is laid out on your bed."

"Sure. Be back soon."

He smiled as Chloe raced out of the room, her long plaited hair trailing behind her.

Amy stood, taking a break from fruit slicing and stretching out her back. "She seems very excited."

"Yes, and she didn't stop to say hello to you. I apologize for her bad manners."

Her smile widened, revealing evenly spaced white teeth. "I'm sure we'll have time to catch up later."

"I'd better go and see my parents. It's nearly time to start greeting our guests. Did you want to take a break now?"

"No, I'm fine. I'd rather finish the fruit first. Please go ahead and I'll keep everything running in here."

"Are you sure?"

She nodded. "I took the liberty of perusing your schedule, and I'll keep all the preparations on track."

"Thank you." He grinned. "I appreciate all your help."

"No problem." She returned to the stool and recommenced her work on the colorful platters.

He left the kitchen and made his way to the front of his home. The door was wide-open and the aroma of barbecuing meat wafted inside. Long tables were set up along the wide veranda that wrapped around two sides of the colonial-style house.

His parents were on the lawn, greeting a dozen guests who had already arrived. Declan had found one of his friends and they were together on the swing set, Lily the dog keeping watch.

He joined his parents, greeting the new arrivals and playing the role of host. He was surprised he hadn't seen Chloe running around in her pretty pink floral dress, a present from her beloved auntie Rachel.

He leaned in close to his mother's ear. "Please excuse me. I've left Amy in the kitchen and I want to check that Chloe is okay."

His mother smiled. "I must remember to thank Amy later for all her help. She's a darling girl."

He nodded. "I'll probably end up spending most of my time before dessert in the kitchen. Let me know if you need anything."

"Of course, but I doubt it. Everything is running smoothly, thanks to you."

He kissed his mother's cheek before heading back inside. He made his way to the kitchen, slowing his pace in the hall.

Chloe's excited voice raised an octave. "Amy, I wanted to talk to you alone, just the two of us."

"Sure." Amy's melodic voice carried into the hall.

"Remember how I told you that secret? I've been praying really hard."

"That's a good idea. I'm glad to hear you've been praying and talking to God."

"Yes, and I've been praying for something really special. Extra, extra special."

"Really? What have you been praying that's so important?"

Ben held his breath. What big secret was his daughter about to reveal? And why was she telling Amy?

"I'm praying really hard that you will become my new mommy."

Amy's cheeks burned and she turned away from Chloe's earnest face. "I don't quite know what to say."

"You're not mad with me?"

She met Chloe's wide eyes, looking as if they could fill with tears any minute. "Of course not. You just took me by surprise."

Ben strode into the kitchen, his eyes narrowed. "Chloe, I overheard what you said to Amy."

Amy lowered her lashes, mortified to know Ben had been listening. How much of the conversation had he overheard?

"Please, Daddy, don't be mad." A big tear plopped out of the corner of Chloe's eye. "You know how much I miss Mommy."

"Come here." He opened his arms and Chloe launched herself against his chest. He bent over and held her close, stroking her hair. "It's okay. I can understand why you'd think Amy would make a great mother."

Amy's breath caught in her throat and her heart constricted. He'd voiced her heart's desire with no idea that having her own children was impossible. She pressed her lips together, determined to keep her rampant emotions in check.

Chloe lifted her head, meeting her father's loving gaze. "Does this mean it will happen?"

He grinned. "No, you cheeky monkey. Sometimes God doesn't answer our prayers the way we want."

"Why not?" She turned to Amy. "What do you think?"

"I agree with your father. Just because we pray really hard for something doesn't mean that God will say yes. Sometimes God has a different plan, but what we do know is that He loves us and listens to our prayers."

Ben nodded. "Amy is right. We can't always get what we want."

Chloe wiped away another tear from her eye. "Did you pray really hard for Mommy to get better when she was really sick?"

His face froze, a sadness pervading his eyes. "Sweetheart, you have no idea how many hours I spent on my knees, begging for your mother to be healed."

Amy blinked, moisture starting to build in her eyes. She could feel Ben's pain as if it had happened only yesterday. Memories of her own loss penetrated her mind.

"But God didn't answer and make Mommy better. Why?"

He sighed, standing up to his full height and holding his daughter's hands. "It wasn't God's plan for your mother to be healed. I'll never know why, and I wish I could give you a different answer."

He turned to Amy, his cloudy eyes pleading for her help.

Amy cleared her throat. "Sometimes God allows bad things to happen. That's why Jesus came, to bring us eternal life and hope because we live in a broken world."

"Too many bad things happen," Chloe said.

She nodded. "We have promises in the Bible that we can hold on to. I believe God has good things planned for us, but sometimes we have to struggle and deal with things that aren't nice. Your mommy is in heaven and you'll get to see her again one day."

Chloe attempted to smile. "I want Mommy to be proud of me. Auntie Rachel says Mommy would be very happy if she could see me and Declan now."

Amy met Ben's gaze and saw raw emotion covering his face. "Your auntie Rachel is a smart lady. You should listen to her."

Chloe turned to her father. "Can I go outside now?"

He nodded. "Be careful you don't ruin your dress."

"I will." Chloe spun on her heel and ran out of the kitchen.

Ben leaned forward, his palms planted on the kitchen counter, head lowered. "I'm sorry."

"It's okay. I understand her desire for a mother. She was very young when she lost her mom, and it must have been very hard for all of you."

He lifted his head, meeting her gaze. "It's encouraging to hear she has finally accepted that Jenny is gone. Although her solution is a bit awkward."

Amy lowered her lashes. "Chloe's a great girl. It's good to hear she's praying."

He nodded. "That would please Jenny. Look, I'm sorry Chloe has pegged you as her new mother. I'm not sure where she got the idea from...."

"No big deal. She'll probably come up with a new idea next week."

"Maybe. Anyway, her behavior is embarrassing and I'll talk to her about it later."

Amy sat back on the stool and resumed cutting the fruit. "She has a good heart."

"And a big mouth." He frowned, his gaze thoughtful. "She is right about one thing."

"Which is?"

"You'll make a great mother one day."

She flinched and the sharp blade of the knife scraped the tip of her index finger.

"Ouch." She ripped a paper towel off a nearby roll, applying pressure to her finger.

"Are you okay?" Ben rushed to her side, his eyes wide.

Blood seeped through the paper towel wrapped tight around her finger.

"I'll find a bandage," he said.

She bit her lip, the sting from the cut starting to recede.

He ferreted in a cupboard behind her, returning with antiseptic spray and a box of waterproof Band-Aids. "Here, let me take a look."

She lifted the paper towel off her finger and a tiny cut oozed blood. "It's only a graze and it should stop bleeding in a minute if I keep applying pressure."

He nodded. "You're the nurse and I'll let you make the decisions."

She attempted a smile. "I hate the antiseptic but it will do the job."

"Yes." He passed over the spray bottle and the package of plastic strips. "What happened? How did you manage to cut your finger?"

"I was careless." She sprayed her fingertip, gritting her teeth to hide her discomfort. She applied the plastic bandage, thankful it was a finger on her left hand. "And you said something that startled me."

He raised an eyebrow. "Now I'm confused."

She held his gaze, digging deep to dredge up the courage to speak the truth. "There's something you don't know. Actually, only a handful of people know."

"Are you okay?"

She nodded, clearing her throat. "I'm fine. Doug and I tried for a couple of years to get pregnant. We tried IVF, but the problem was with me." She looked him straight in the eye. "I can never have children of my own."

Chapter 8

Ben's jaw dropped, his mind spinning. Amy couldn't have children. Her words echoed in his head and he felt as though he'd been punched hard in the stomach.

Amy loved kids and she was so good with his children. Her eyes shone with her pain.

"Amy, I don't know what to say. I had no idea...."

"I've had to accept it, and, as I said, very few people know about it." She examined her bandaged finger, her voice shaky. "I've found people tend to assume I was waiting until I was older to have children."

"That makes sense." It had never crossed his mind to question his assumption that she could one day give birth to her own children.

She blinked, her gaze fixed on the fruit platter. "My friends were planning to have families in their thirties because it's expensive to live in Sydney."

"Jenny always wanted to have children and we had no reason to wait." In hindsight it had been a good decision and he had no regrets.

She lifted her head, meeting his gaze. "It's good Chloe and Declan were old enough to remember their mother."

He nodded. He couldn't imagine his life without his children. Would they start to forget Jenny as their memories faded? He should visit Sunny Ridge more often so they could spend time with Jenny's family.

He opened the fridge, removing two large salad bowls. He was blessed to have Chloe and Declan, and Jenny's memory lived on in his children. But Amy didn't have that comfort.

Empathy filled his heart along with an acknowledgment that Amy understood the loneliness and emptiness he had experienced.

"Are you ready for lunch?" He closed the fridge door with his elbow. "I think we're on top of everything and have earned a break."

She nodded. "I'd prefer to eat lunch here and clean up my mess."

"Sure. I'll take the salads out now and bring back our lunch."

She told him her food preferences and he left the kitchen with the salads. He chatted with guests outside, where a buffet-style long table was set up in the middle section of the veranda. The atmosphere was jovial and children's laughter carried through the air.

He was happy his parents had reached this milestone in their marriage, but a hint of disappointment pierced his heart. His dream of growing old with Jenny had been shattered. It had taken time to accept her loss and move on.

He squared his shoulders, determined to enjoy the party and not allow his melancholy over his own short marriage to ruin his day. Thankful for Amy's help, he filled two plates with food and returned to the kitchen. Amy had cleared away all the fruit scraps and set two places at the table.

She smiled. "That smells good." She slipped into a seat at the table.

He passed over her plate. "Enjoy."

"I will." She paused. "Can I please say grace?"

He sat next to her. "Go ahead."

"Lord, thanks for this food and party to celebrate Ben's parents' anniversary. Amen."

"Amen." He sampled his steak, the tender beef melting in his mouth.

She tasted his salad. "I'm impressed. The dressing has a Thai flavor."

He grinned. "I'm not giving away clues."

"Not even a tiny little one?"

"Nope."

She pretended to pout and his smile widened. Amy was fun to be around, and he was glad she had agreed to help him in the kitchen. He looked forward to spending time with her over lunch.

Amy stood in the far back corner of the veranda, her parents seated a few feet in front of her at a long table. She listened to Ben's father's speech and laughed along with friends and family at his humorous anecdotes from forty years of marriage.

Ben's parents held hands and were surrounded by their children and grandchildren at the central point of the veranda. The color on Ben's cheekbones rose as his parents described Ben's early attempt, at age six, to fix a broken-down tractor by dismantling part of the engine.

She smiled. His mechanical aptitude had shown at a young age. He stepped forward and gave a short but moving speech about the positive role his parents had played in his life and the lives of his children. She blinked, his kind words seeping into her soul as he thanked his parents for the extra help they provided for his kids.

His tender gaze landed on her and his eyes held hers for a long moment, an unspoken message of thanks communicated in a simple look. Her pulse raced and she lowered her lashes, breaking their connection. He acknowledged the contributions of the people who had helped make his parents' party a special day before stepping aside for Luke to take his turn.

She looked up and found Ben's gaze remained fixed on her. Her lips curved into a smile and he winked.

She drew in a deep breath. Their relationship was moving into uncharted territory and a flicker of hope lit in her heart. Did she deserve a second chance at love? Was it possible that God could answer her prayers and provide her with a family to love?

Doubts and insecurities plagued her mind. Doug had blamed her for their difficult marriage. Her inability to provide children and meet all his needs had driven him to seek his pleasure elsewhere. His fatal diving holiday in the Maldives might not have taken place if he'd been happy to spend time with her.

Guilt, her familiar friend, ate away at her heart. Ben was too good for her. He'd shared an amazing marriage with Jenny, and her shoes were way too big for Amy to consider filling.

She wrapped her arms around her torso, the light breeze bringing out goose bumps on her arms. Luke was wrong. Ben would soon realize that she wasn't capable of meeting his needs and making him happy. She valued their friendship but acknowledged the bitter truth she couldn't ignore.

She swallowed hard, her stomach clenched in a tight

knot. It was only a matter of time before Ben realized she wasn't the right woman for him.

Amy tucked a loose strand of hair behind her ears. The wind had picked up and she was glad she wore sunglasses to prevent dust from blowing into her eyes. Chloe and Declan played on the swings, less than twenty feet away. Amy lounged back on the wooden bench seat, the hard slats uncomfortable against her spine. After a hectic Saturday morning at the clinic, she was grateful to sit down and have some time to herself.

Two weeks had passed since the party at Ben's house. She questioned whether she should have shared with Ben the details of her fertility issues. Their friendship had grown to a point where she felt comfortable talking with him about almost anything. Except the closely guarded truth of her marriage. She couldn't bear for him to learn how badly she'd failed Doug.

Footsteps sounded behind her and she shivered, wrapping her scarf closer around her neck.

"Amy."

She tensed, the deep grating voice accentuating her discomfort. What was he doing here? Following her?

Jed sat close beside her and she instinctively shrank away to the edge of the bench, her gaze fixed on the kids in the playground.

"You're not even going to say hello?"

She shuddered. "What do you want?"

Jed turned to face her. "Is everything fixed at your house?"

She averted her gaze. "Yes. I don't need any more work done."

"That's a shame. I don't have a lot of work scheduled this week."

Not her problem. She leaned away from him, her gaze

remaining steady on Chloe and Declan. If only one of the kids would call her over and give her an excuse to get away from him.

He shuffled closer. "Did you get my phone messages?"

She stood, unable to sit any longer with him inching toward her. "Yes, but I'm too busy to call you."

"Busy doing what?"

"Stuff." She crossed her arms over her chest. Her life was none of his business.

"I thought we could go to the movies again."

She shivered, her stomach churning. "I don't think so, and please don't call me again." She walked toward the playground.

"Amy, wait." He grabbed her forearm and she wrenched out of his grasp.

"Don't touch me."

Jed raised his hands, a half smile curling up his thin mouth. "Can we talk?"

"I have nothing to say. Leave me alone."

He followed her around the perimeter of the playground. "Why won't you talk to me?"

She stopped, thrusting her hands on her hips. "Have you forgotten what happened when we were driving home from Sunny Ridge?"

"You got the wrong idea."

"I don't think so. You were never going to be able to talk me into going back to your place."

He puffed out his chest. "You didn't give me a chance to explain."

"Explain what, exactly?" She jutted her chin, an icy tone entering her voice. "I'm not a naive teen."

"No, you're not." Ben appeared beside her, sweat glistening on his red face. "Amy, is everything okay?"

"Yes." She glared at Jed. "He was just leaving."

Ben took three steps toward Jed, his piercing gaze riveted to the man's pale face. "What's your name? Ned?"

"Jed. And what's it to you?"

"The lady asked you to leave her alone."

Jed shuffled from one foot to the other, seeming to weigh his options. "I think I get the picture." He turned to Amy. "Why didn't you tell me you were with him?"

She gasped.

Ben stood taller. "Because what she does in her personal life isn't your concern."

"Okay, mate, no need to get worked up. I'm out of here." Jed sauntered away, as if he didn't have a care in the world.

Ben turned to her, his mouth a grim line. "He's the guy who left you stranded that night, isn't he?"

Ben clenched his fists, adrenaline coursing through muscles warm from running around during the first half of the game.

"I think he got the message." Amy nibbled on her lower lip. "You should go back to the game, especially since your team is winning."

He shook his head. "I'm not going anywhere." He returned Chloe's wave and his daughter gave a big whoop as she slid feetfirst down the slide.

Amy's eyes widened. "But doesn't your team need you?"

He shrugged. "I'm not playing the second half. For a change we actually have a couple of reserve players who need a run."

He'd been distracted by Amy trying to get rid of Jed. The ball had slid through his fingers more than once, and he didn't object when Jack, his team captain, suggested he sit out the second half.

She sighed. "I really don't think he'll be back or try to bother me again."

"He better not or he'll have to deal with me." His protective instincts were on full alert. The moment Jed had touched Amy's arm, the urge to intervene had intensified. He'd been thankful when the halftime whistle blew, allowing a quick conversation with Jack before running over to help Amy.

He frowned. "How did you get tangled up with Jed?"

"I ran into him in town a few days after I moved back."

"Has he been bothering you again?"

"He left a couple of messages on my phone this week, which I ignored. Believe it or not, we were friends at school."

"But not anymore."

"I wonder what happened to him. He's so desperate and lonely."

He raised an eyebrow. "Don't you start feeling sorry for him, after what he did to you."

"I can't help feeling a bit sad." She flicked her ponytail over her shoulder. "Jed had plans to leave town, get an education. His home life was difficult, but he achieved good grades at school. Something obviously went wrong."

"Life happens and we're forced to deal with the real world." The curveballs seemed to hit some people harder than others.

"Yep. I'll try to remember to pray for him."

He narrowed his eyes. "Don't forget you can forgive someone without putting yourself back in harm's way."

"I know, and stop worrying. I can take care of myself."

"So you tell me."

She smiled. "Are you thirsty? I have a spare bottle of chilled water in my bag."

"Thanks. That sounds great." He'd left his nearly empty drink bottle on the far side of the field.

She passed him the water and his fingertips slid over the back of her hand. A jolt of awareness shot through him and he held her warm gaze. He couldn't deny any longer that his feelings for Amy were developing into something more than friendship.

He dipped his head back and gulped down half the water.

She laughed. "You sure were thirsty."

He nodded. "It's thirsty work, running around the field."

"Your sprint down the sideline to score was pretty impressive."

He grinned. "You were watching?"

"Yep. Declan was very excited, and he even clapped for his daddy."

His heart swelled. "My boy loves his football." He was thrilled to hear that she'd also paid attention to the game. His awareness of her had intensified since she'd bared her heart and shared her infertility anguish at his parents' anniversary party. He'd kept one eye on Amy and the other on the ball, explaining his erratic performance before the halftime break when Jack had pulled him aside to ask what was wrong.

Rachel was in Sunny Ridge this afternoon and he appreciated Amy's willingness to supervise his kids. Amy had become the unofficial babysitter of the players' kids, and she knew many of them from the children's program at church.

He glanced at his watch. "I'm taking the kids out for ice cream after the game, if you're interested in coming along?"

"The usual ice-cream shop?"

He nodded. "The one you tell me you love way too much."

"Okay." She wiped her hands on the sides of her fitted jeans. "I can only indulge because I was good and went to the gym this week."

"Your ice-cream rules are exhausting." He grinned. "The only decision I make is single or double cone."

"You work outdoors and are physically active in the orchards. And you play football every week. My job is sedentary and I have to watch what I eat these days."

He took in her slim physique, with curves in all the right places. "You look fine to me."

"I think I'll stick to frozen yogurt today."

"No triple chocolate?"

She met his gaze, her eyes gleaming. "Don't tempt me. You're not playing fair because you've probably burned off at least three ice creams during the game."

"You could always participate like Rachel and earn your ice cream."

She wrinkled her nose. "Trust me, my ball skills are not good enough to be on public display. I'll stick to hanging out with the kids."

"Fair enough." He'd fallen into the habit of having ice cream with Rachel after the game, and Amy had started tagging along. This would be the first week Amy joined him and the kids without his sister.

He smiled. "I'll grab my gear now and we can take off a little early."

"Sure. I'll organize the kids and find someone to supervise the other kids in the park."

"Did you drive here today?"

She shook her head. "I need the exercise, remember?" She threw him a bright smile over her shoulder before walking over to the slide, her hips gently swaying.

He dropped his gaze, reining in thoughts that hadn't lingered in his head since he'd become a single dad. An ice-cream date with Amy was a temptation too big to resist.

Chapter 9

Amy parked in her usual spot under a gum tree at the back of Ben's house. Chloe was making excellent progress with her piano lessons, and it seemed she'd inherited her mother's musical talent. She'd also proved diligent in her music practice during the week, unlike Amy at the same age. Amy's piano teacher had despaired that she'd never progress because she didn't make practice time a priority.

She drained the remainder of her lukewarm latte and stashed the empty cup in her car before heading toward the house. Declan rode his bike along the gravel drive.

She waved in greeting. "Hey, Declan, how are you doing?"

He braked hard, pulling the bike to a stop in front of her. "I'm training to do a long ride." His flushed face glowed in the late-afternoon sunlight. "Uncle Luke has promised to take me on a real ride through the pine forest soon."

She smiled. "Sounds like fun. How far will you be riding?"

"Don't know. Uncle Luke wants to drive to the main track into the forest."

"A good idea." Her gaze swept the yard. "Is Chloe inside?"

He nodded. "Dad said he wanted to see you."

She lifted a brow. "Now, or after Chloe's lesson?"

"Not sure." He tapped his finger on his chin. "Dad's fixing something in the shed."

"Okay, I'll go find him. Have fun riding."

"I will." Declan rode away and she made her way to a large tin shed where Ben stored a range of machinery and equipment. He had been an auto mechanic in Sunny Ridge before moving back to Snowgum Creek and taking over the family orchards.

She walked to the entrance. A white Jaguar was on a hoist in the middle of the shed.

Ben smiled. "Is it four-thirty already?"

"I'm ten minutes early."

He wore an old shirt, streaked with grease, and ripped jeans. His casual attire and tousled hair accentuated his good looks.

He wiped his hands on a cloth. "I'll be back inside soon, once I work out what's wrong with the transmission."

She widened her eyes. "I didn't know you owned a Jag."

"It's not mine. Jack bought it to add to his wedding-car fleet, and he asked me to check a few things."

She smiled. "It's nice that you're helping him out. Do you think there's something seriously wrong with the Jag?"

"I'm not sure yet. Jack knows a lot about cars and does his own maintenance. He only ever sends them to me if he thinks there's a major problem."

"Okay." She walked around the car, admiring the leather interior and polished finish. The paintwork was in immaculate condition. "How old is the car?"

"It's a 1970s model with one owner who looked after it.

Apparently he only sold it because he was ninety-two and no longer able to pass his driver's-license test."

"Wow. It sounds like the car has a fascinating history."

He nodded. "The mileage is very low for its age. The car was mainly used for touring, and it was garaged nearly all the time, away from the coast."

She peered at the paintwork. "I can't see any rust at all. My previous car suffered in Sydney from the salty sea air, even though it was garaged most of the time."

"What did you drive?"

She paused, hesitating to admit she had driven a luxury car, as befitting the wife of a top Sydney doctor from an old-money family. "A BMW."

His eyebrows shot up. "A new Beemer shouldn't have rusted."

"It was parked outdoors a lot while I attended classes at university." She sighed. "I spent a fair bit of time near the water." The beach and parklands surrounding the harbor foreshores had been her escape, a haven away from her troubles at home.

"Makes sense. Have you checked your current car for rust?"

She shook her head. "I've only had it a few months. My previous car, the one I bought after trading in the BMW, came to a sad end."

"Really? Were you in an accident?"

"No, a tree branch fell on it during a storm, crushing the roof."

He gasped. "Were you in the car at the time?"

"I was at work on night shift, and I'd parked on a sub-urban street near the hospital because the staff car park was full. I'd been praying about moving back to Snowgum Creek, and the car fiasco was the final straw that sealed my decision."

He frowned. "I imagine you weren't too happy to find your car decimated."

She nodded. "I was bleary-eyed after a long night shift, and all I had wanted to do was drive home and curl up in bed. The following weekend I listed my apartment with a real-estate agent and applied for the job my mother had told me about at Luke's clinic."

"It seems like coming back here was a good move for you."

"I think so. By the way, Declan said you wanted to see me."

He looked her straight in the eye, his gaze warm. "Do you have dinner plans tonight?"

"No, unless you count the leftovers I was planning to reheat in the microwave."

"Would you like to stay and have dinner with us? I'm making a pasta sauce, nothing fancy."

Her heart skipped a beat and she smiled. "Sounds great. I've heard from Rachel and Luke that you make great pasta."

He dipped his head. "We usually eat around six. I'll have to make sure Chloe completes her homework before dinner."

"Sure." She glanced at her watch. "I'll go up to the house now for Chloe's lesson before she sends out a search party. Thanks for the invite."

His smile widened, accentuating a dimple in his cheek. "No worries. I'll be finished here soon."

She nodded before turning to leave the shed. What was it about Ben that drew her to him like a magnet with an irresistible force?

Amy swallowed her last mouthful of pasta sauce, the aromatic flavors satisfying her taste buds.

Ben smiled. "Would you like seconds?"

She shook her head. "This is perfect, thank you."

Chloe's cutlery clattered on her plate. "Daddy, can I leave the table now?"

"Not if you're planning to watch television."

"But, Dad—"

"No buts. It's a school day tomorrow and you need to get ready for bed. Did you borrow a new book to read from the school library?"

Chloe nodded. "I found the second-last book in the Narnia series."

"Excellent," Ben said.

Declan yawned, covering his mouth with his hand.

"Amy, please excuse us. I think it's bedtime for both of them."

"Sure. I'll clean up while you organize the children."

"You don't need to do that. I can clean up later."

"No big deal. It's the least I can do." She stood, wishing the children good-night before clearing the dishes from the table. Ben herded his children down the hall in the direction of their bedrooms.

She packed the dishwasher and found a stash of hot-chocolate sachets on the kitchen counter.

Before long, Ben returned to the kitchen.

"Are they asleep already?"

"Not yet, but they're settled. Declan can barely keep his eyes open and Chloe will probably read for a while."

"Tea or hot chocolate?"

He smiled. "Definitely hot chocolate, but let me make it since you've done all the cleaning up."

"Okay." She stood back while he heated mugs of milk in the microwave. Within minutes they walked through to the family room. She slipped off her shoes and sank back into his sofa, tucking her feet underneath her and holding her mug with both hands.

He settled in an overstuffed lounge recliner opposite the television.

She lifted a brow. "Is this your nighttime routine?"

He nodded. "Very boring, I know."

"Do you read?"

"Mainly action books and thrillers. Luke often lends me books from his collection."

She sipped her drink, the milk warming her throat.

"By the way, I meant to tell you that your mother is looking really well. My mother told me she has the all clear."

She smiled. "The cancer is gone and it's such a relief. She'll still be monitored because it could return, but her prognosis is good."

"I'm glad she's doing well."

She gasped, covering her mouth with her hand. "Oh, Ben, I'm sorry. I know this is a sensitive topic for you."

He shrugged. "It's okay to talk about it. I am sorry Jenny didn't make it, but I'm also glad when other people do. Modern medicine works for some cancer sufferers, and others aren't so lucky."

She drew her brows together. "I don't know if it relates to luck."

"I've found no other explanation. I struggled for three years to understand why God took Jenny, and came up empty. Well-meaning people have tried to tell me it's part of God's plan, but they have no answers when I ask why it was God's plan for my children to grow up without their mother."

The pain in his voice reverberated around the cozy room. Her throat tightened and she remembered the fear she'd experienced when her father had called her with news of her mother's cancer diagnosis. The phone had slipped through her fingers, the screen cracking on her tiled kitchen floor. Doug had later chastised her for her carelessness, seemingly unaware of and not caring about the incredible well of emotion bubbling inside her.

She cleared her throat. "Have you spoken with my father?"

He nodded. "He was very helpful, probably because of what he was going through personally with your mother's situation."

"It's hard, especially for young kids, to understand. It was tough for me to face the prospect of losing my mom, but I'm an adult with the ability and maturity to cope with the situation."

He sipped his hot chocolate. "They're getting there, but it's not an easy journey. It never crossed my mind years ago that I'd end up being a single parent and raising my kids on my own."

"You've done a good job. Chloe and Declan are lovely kids."

"It helps having my family close by. My parents and siblings play an important role in their lives."

She nodded. "I'd like to see my sister more often."

"I heard she was living in Sunny Ridge?"

"Bella moved there a few years ago after her wedding." They had drifted apart after Amy had left home and moved to Sydney. Her sister had rebelled against her religious upbringing in her late teens, creating a lot of heartache for their parents. Bella did attend church in Snowgum Creek at Christmas and Easter, but had admitted to Amy that she did it only to pacify their father.

"Do you see her often?"

She shook her head. "She lives her own life, and the five-year age gap hasn't helped. Bella was still at school when I moved to Sydney."

"I'd forgotten that she's a lot younger than you."

"My mom also struggled with fertility issues, hence the

big age gap." Her mother had suffered numerous miscar-
riages and other problems.

"I'm sorry to hear this."

She nodded. Her yearning for a baby, for her own children to love, wouldn't die. *Lord, please help me to accept
my lot in life and to learn to be content with my current
circumstances.*

Amy rubbed her hands over her face, her eyes fatigued.
It was only midmorning. She'd stayed up late last night
watching a movie with Rachel and was paying for it today.

She stifled a yawn. The phone on her desk rang and she
reached for the handset, the distinctive ringtone signaling
an external call.

"Hello, Amy speaking."

"Hey, Amy, I'm glad I caught you between patients."
Ben's rich voice resonated through the handset.

She smiled. "It's not too hard to catch me today. I'm having a slow Friday morning."

"That's unusual."

"Yep, but I'm making the most of it and catching up
on admin."

"Good idea." He paused. "Do you have lunch plans?"

She widened her eyes. "No. I have patients scheduled
until twelve-thirty, assuming they all turn up on time, then
a gap until two."

"I'm heading into town soon. Would you like to go out
for lunch?"

"Sure." Her pulse raced. She was thankful she'd brought
her makeup bag to work and had time to fix her weary face
before their lunch date.

"I'll meet you at the clinic."

"Or I can meet you somewhere." She swallowed the last
mouthful of her tepid instant coffee and wrinkled her nose.
She needed a real coffee soon.

"I can be at the clinic by twelve-thirty."

"What did you have in mind?" She could avoid being interrogated by Luke if they met elsewhere. The knowing look her boss would inflict on her if he heard about their lunch plans was something she'd be happy to avoid.

"Not sure yet. Maybe we could go to the café where you buy your coffee."

"Sounds great." Her mouth watered at the prospect of decent coffee. "I'll meet you there when I can escape from here."

He chuckled. "You make it sound like you're in prison."

"Sometimes it feels like it." She looked at the time on her computer screen. "I have to go. See you soon."

She ended the call and tucked a few loose strands of hair behind her ears. With any luck, she'd be out the door and drinking the latte she desperately needed by twelve-thirty.

At twenty past twelve she led her last patient before lunch into the reception area. An earlier cancellation had put her ahead of schedule.

Ben leaned on the doorframe at the entrance to his brother's consulting room, talking with Luke. His lips curved up into a big smile. "Hi, Amy."

She walked over to Ben, careful to dodge Luke's curious gaze. "You're early."

He shrugged. "I got everything done faster than I expected."

Luke grinned. "And here I thought Ben had stopped by to see me."

"Well, I did, and I got lucky because you were between patients."

Heat rose in her cheeks. "Speaking of patients, Mrs. Jones is walking up the path now."

"Yes, she's next on my list," Luke said.

Ben stepped toward her. "Are you waiting for another patient?"

She shook her head. "I'll fetch my purse." She turned to Luke. "And I'll be back by two."

Luke's smile widened. "Take your time. Your appointment at two was postponed until four, so there's no need to rush back."

She cringed. "You don't pay me to have a lunch break." Luke was enjoying himself way too much for her liking.

Ben grinned. "She'll be back on time."

"Have fun." Luke waved and walked over to the reception desk.

She met Ben's gaze. "My purse is in my room."

"Okay." He walked with her while she retrieved her purse, said goodbye to Janice and headed outside.

The bright midday sunshine warmed her skin. She stopped at the bottom of the path. "Are we driving or walking?"

"Is it okay if we walk? My truck needs a good clean and I don't want your clothes ruined."

"Sure." She slipped her sunglasses onto her nose. "It's a nice day for a walk."

She fell into step beside him, her ponytail swinging behind her in the light breeze. "What do you feel like eating?"

"Don't know. Maybe a meat pie or a meatball roll. Since the weather is good, I was thinking we could buy takeout and eat in the park."

"Good idea." She looked forward to sitting on a bench under a shady tree. The gardens were in full bloom, and she enjoyed looking at the colorful flower displays.

They reached the café and joined the lunchtime queue. Doris, her mother's elderly friend and Jack's aunt, waited in front of them.

"Hello, Ben, Amy," Doris said. "Lovely day outside."

Amy nodded. "Good to see you. You're looking well."

"Yes, this old gal still has some life left in her. Amy, I'm so pleased to hear your mother's health update. It must lift a big burden off your shoulders."

She smiled. "We're all relieved she's doing so well."

"And, Ben," Doris said. "I had a lovely time at your parents' anniversary party last month. You all put a lot of work into that party, and there was such a big turnout."

He nodded. "We're glad you could make it. It was a good day."

"Luke and Jack did well to grill such beautiful, tender meat for the large number of guests."

"Yes, they were kept busy," he said.

She shuffled forward in the queue. Doris was next in line to be served.

"I'm buying a sandwich to take back to the community store." Doris smiled. "I slept in late and didn't have time to make my lunch."

"Do you volunteer all day?" she asked.

"Only on Fridays. I sometimes cover Thursday mornings and a few hours on Saturday. If business is slow, I can quilt while I'm in the store."

"Good idea," she said. Doris made beautiful Australian-themed quilts that had won awards.

"And I'm partial to the cappuccinos they make here."

Ben nodded. "Amy assures me this is the place in town to buy coffee."

"She's right." Doris placed her order and moved to a seat on the far side of the waiting area.

Ben turned to Amy. "What would you like?"

She drew her brows together, scanning the takeout items listed on a colorful chalkboard. "A salad roll with ranch dressing will do me."

"And a large latte."

"Of course. One sugar, please."

Ben stepped forward to the front of the queue. He placed their order and insisted on paying.

She stood with Ben near the café entrance, nodding and smiling at the townsfolk milling around and waiting for their food.

She whispered in his ear. "I could have paid for my lunch."

He lowered his voice, his words for her alone. "When I ask a lady out to lunch, it's my responsibility to take care of the details."

Her heart warmed and she dipped her head, hiding the moisture building in her eyes. It had been a very long time since a man had made her feel special by using a few well-chosen and heartfelt words. This lunch was turning out to be so much more than she'd anticipated. How could she possibly resist his charm?

Chapter 10

Amy swallowed the last bite of her delicious salad roll. She tossed the paper bag and wrapping into a nearby bin.

Ben grinned. "Good throw."

She sat up straighter on the bench seat. "Your turn."

He scrunched up the paper wrapping from his meatball roll and lined up his target. The ball of paper landed in the middle of the bin.

"Well done." She sipped her latte. "What are you up to in the orchards?"

"Praying we don't get hail before we pick the crop at the end of the season." He crossed his jeans-clad legs at his ankles, leaning back into the bench seat.

"Do you have a large crop?"

He nodded. "It's been a good season so far. If I can keep the birds away, the animals away, we'll do okay."

"Animals?"

"The kangaroos cause chaos when a herd decides to take a shortcut through the orchards. I spotted an emu the other day. And the wombats dig holes too close to the tree roots or in the middle of the track between the rows."

"Don't forget the snakes." She shivered. "I freak out whenever I see the skin they've shed lying around."

"I can coexist with the snakes who eat vermin and don't mess with the apple trees." He sipped his coffee. "As long as you leave them alone, they won't cause you any harm."

She frowned. "I've had too many close encounters with poisonous snakes to feel relaxed knowing they are anywhere near me. I wear hiking boots in summer if I'm outdoors and in a snake-prone area."

He chuckled. "You need to relax. When Chloe was two or three, she kicked what she thought was a brown tree branch in our back garden at Sunny Ridge. But the branch moved and she ran screaming into the house."

"Poor girl. She must have been petrified."

"It took Jenny hours to console her, and she didn't disobey her mother again by sneaking outside without permission. I saw that snake a couple of times, but it had gone into hiding by the time we called the ranger out to catch it."

"Ugh, I'm all spooked now. I have a regular gardening service that keeps my lawn short and the yard clear of nice hiding places for snakes."

"You don't mow your own lawns?"

She wrinkled her nose. "I get hay fever from cut grass. So far I've survived this spring without any major problems."

"I didn't know you suffered from hay fever."

"You don't remember what happened when I was twelve or thirteen?"

He shook his head.

"The grass-clippings fight at the farm, boys versus girls?"

"Hey, that wasn't my idea. I think Luke was settling a score with Rachel."

"Is that how you remember it?"

"I know Luke got in a lot of trouble."

"My mother called your mother, because I had two days off school due to eyes that oozed gunk and were nearly swollen shut."

"Oh, Amy, I had no idea. I'm sorry if I threw grass in your eyes."

She smiled. "It's okay. By memory I think Rachel enjoyed getting Luke into trouble way too much."

"What's new? It's interesting that they can happily live under the same roof now, because they used to fight all the time when they were kids."

"I remember." She drained her cup, savoring the last few drops of her coffee. "I should probably get back to work soon."

"We have time for a walk around the park first, if you're interested."

She stood, stretching out the kinks in her back. "Sounds good. I'm glad I wore my comfy shoes today."

He tossed his coffee cup in the bin. "That was good coffee."

"You'll have to invest in a coffeemaker and buy ground coffee instead of instant."

He raised an eyebrow and started walking beside her. "I don't drink it enough to warrant the effort."

"I'll have to convert you."

"Good luck." He laughed. "You wouldn't be the first person to try."

"But I play to win." Ben was getting a coffeemaker and a large packet of ground coffee from her for Christmas, whether he liked it or not.

They walked through the rose garden, where a couple of varieties were in full bloom. They passed the flower beds of bulbs, including tulips that were past ready to be topped and dug out for next year. It seemed as though the town gardener had fallen behind schedule.

He paused in front of a garden bed with colorful pansies and petunias, turning to meet her gaze. "Have I mentioned I've been invited to a wedding?"

She shook her head. "Sounds fun. Where's it being held?"

"Sunny Ridge. One of the mechanics I used to work with who also went to our church is finally getting hitched."

"Do you know his fiancée?"

"She was friends with Jenny."

"It sounds like a great opportunity to catch up with old friends."

He nodded. "I should visit Sunny Ridge more often, but it's hard with the kids at school and their weekend activities."

"True. I'd like to go back to Sydney sometime to see my friends, but I rarely have two days off in a row."

"I'm sure Luke would give you the leave if you asked."

"Yes, but there's no one else available to fill in odd days, and his schedule is already overloaded. I'm taking a couple of weeks off work in January. The clinic is traditionally quieter during the summer school holidays and Luke won't need to replace me."

"Good idea. Anyway, I need to RSVP tomorrow for the wedding. The ceremony will be held at four in the afternoon at my old church before a dinner reception at the manor house outside Sunny Ridge with the English name I always forget."

"Yes, I know the venue." The manicured grounds around the nineteenth-century mansion were known for their spectacular rose gardens.

"I'm leaving the children overnight with my parents. Would you like to come to the wedding with me?"

She widened her eyes. "Which date is it?"

"The second Saturday in December, just over three weeks away."

She chewed her lip, mentally reviewing her calendar.

She hadn't picked up any extra shifts at the hospital during December. "Yes, I'd love to go. I'll make sure I can leave the clinic by twelve on that Saturday."

His smile widened. "Great. I'll RSVP tonight."

"What's the dress code?"

"Semiformal." He grimaced. "I'll suffer through the heat in a suit and tie."

She lifted a brow. "We may get lucky and have a cooler day. I have a couple of dresses that I could wear."

"I'm sure you'll look fabulous in whatever you wear."

She lowered her lashes, heat rising up her neck. The wedding provided an opportunity for Ben to introduce her to his friends who knew Jenny. She sucked in a steadying breath, hoping his friends would like her and that she would compare favorably to his late wife. It had been ages since she'd last dressed up for an event, and she looked forward to spending an evening with Ben.

Ben parked his car in the last available space in the Sunny Ridge Community Church lot and switched off the engine.

Amy glanced at the crowd of wedding guests milling outside the church. "I'm glad we aren't late."

"Yes, I knew there would be a big turnout. I'll help you out of the car." He strolled around the front of the car to the passenger side.

Her breath caught in her throat. He looked amazing in a suit, his broad shoulders filling out the tailored charcoal jacket.

Ben opened her door, and she swung around in her seat, ready to step out of the car. The skirt of her long dress glided over her legs. Her pale pink silk dress, with beading on the bodice and delicate spaghetti straps, complemented her fair complexion.

She smiled. Ben had drawn the line at wearing a pink

shirt or tie to coordinate with her dress. She adjusted a hair-
pin near her ear. Secured in an updo, her hairstyle was a
soft version of a French roll that wasn't going to give her a
headache by the end of the evening.

He held out his hand. "Are you ready?"

She placed her hand in his, electric tingles shooting up
her arm. Her awareness of him intensified as she stood beside him, his calloused hand gently enfolding hers.

His eyes twinkled. "Let's do it."

She nodded. Hand firmly enclosed in his, she walked
beside him to the church. The uneven gravel parking lot
wasn't easy to negotiate in two-inch heels.

He slowed his pace. "Are you okay?"

"I'll be okay once I'm on even ground. I don't want to
scuff my heels."

She stopped walking and lifted her left knee, adjust-
ing the strap at the back of her ankle. "That feels better."

"Your shoes look expensive."

"Don't ask how much I paid. I bought them to wear
with this dress."

He raised an eyebrow. "How many pairs of shoes do
you own?"

"You're better off not knowing the answer to that question." She smiled. "Although your sister is saving money
because she borrows my shoes."

"You're right. I don't want to know." They approached
the church entrance, and Ben leaned closer, whispering in
her ear. "You'll probably know a few people, and nearly
everyone will know your father."

"The downside of being a pastor's kid."

He squeezed her hand. "You'll be fine."

She pasted a bright smile on her face, ready to greet the
guests. A number of people who looked vaguely familiar
gave her and Ben quizzical looks. The warmth from his
hand was comforting and reassuring. And empowering.

She was no longer the neglected wife of a high-flying doctor. No longer the object of pity at social gatherings and blatantly snubbed by her former in-laws at family events.

She straightened her spine, glad to have Ben close by her side as she failed to remember the names of people who recognized her. His helpful use of their names jogged her memory. He was right. They all seemed to know her father and the good news about her mother's recovery from cancer.

Ben pulled her aside, his eyes sparkling. "We should head into the church now and find a seat."

"Sure." She followed his lead, and they found two seats toward the back near the center aisle.

Right on time, the bride entered the church and commenced her long walk down the aisle to her future husband. Her vintage bridal gown, with ivory lace detail and a long train, looked stunning. Her radiant face glowed under her veil in the afternoon sunlight streaming through the beautiful stained-glass windows. The church was bigger than the one in Snowgum Creek and full to capacity. It seemed as if the whole town had turned out to watch the wedding ceremony.

She stood with Ben for the opening song. His hand rested lightly on her waist, the palm imprint warming her skin through her silk dress. He held the order-of-service booklet they shared so that she could see the words to the hymn, his rich voice blending with the congregation as they all sang.

She mumbled the unfamiliar words, inhaling Ben's distinctive citrus-scented aftershave. It was weird to know he used to attend services at this church every Sunday. In a different life. He'd seemed comfortable here, chatting with old friends before the ceremony.

The song ended and she took her seat, aware that Ben was only inches away from her.

She switched her focus back to the ceremony, too distracted by the gorgeous man beside her. He had drawn a number of admiring glances from female guests of all ages, his dark wavy hair curling above his collar. His hair seemed to effortlessly look good, unlike the hours she spent styling her own temperamental mane.

The short Bible readings completed, the senior pastor moved to the podium to give his talk. He was a good friend of her father's, and she had briefly chatted with him and his wife at the anniversary party. The pastor centered his talk on love and commitment, no big surprise for a wedding ceremony.

The pastor reminded the couple of their Biblical marriage roles. He talked about a husband's responsibility to love his wife, and how that would look using real-life examples.

Her heart squeezed tight, the familiar feelings of rejection and unworthiness rising to the surface. She tensed, the words resonating in her head. Was she wrong to blame herself for Doug's lack of unconditional love? Had it ever crossed his mind to try to love her in the same way that Christ loved the church?

The Apostle Paul's analogy of Jesus as the bridegroom and the church his bride captured her attention in a new way. Jesus had given his life for the church. Doug had rarely sacrificed or compromised his needs for her benefit.

How could she walk away from the guilt and release her resentment and anger, the negative emotions she had repressed because Doug was gone and she was left behind to pick up the pieces?

She sneaked a sideways glance at Ben, his gaze intent on the pastor at the front. He was a man who continually showed he cared about her needs. A man she was starting to fall for, big-time. He'd slowly broken through her emotional defenses, and their friendship had evolved into something more.

A big question plagued her mind. Where did they go from here? Everyone she knew had an incredibly high opinion of Jenny. How could she measure up, after he'd experienced a near-perfect marriage with a woman loved by all?

Her insecurities resurfaced. It was only a matter of time until he realized she couldn't compete with the legend of Jenny. She'd make the most of whatever happiness she could find now because it was inevitable he'd work out the truth. And shatter her heart into a million tiny little pieces in the process.

Amy spooned the remainder of her crème brûlée into her mouth, savoring the sweet flavors. The last speech, a long but humorous one by the best man, was wound up by the master of ceremonies. The bridal couple danced the traditional waltz under a spotlight in the center of the room.

A dreamy smile tilted up her lips. The newlywed couple was obviously very much in love and looking forward to the next stage of their lives together. Ben had introduced her to the happy couple before dessert, and she had appreciated their warm welcome.

Ben cleared his throat. "I have a confession."

She lifted a brow. "This sounds intriguing." They were seated at a round table at the back of the large ballroom. A light breeze carried cool air into the room from the open French doors behind their table.

"I'm a terrible dancer."

She laughed. "Most men are."

"Hey, you're not being very nice."

"It's okay. I have to concentrate to dance in heels this high, and I'm out of practice."

"We can dance if you really want to." He grinned, lowering his voice. "Or we could duck outside and check out the gardens."

She glanced through the inviting open French doors. Strategically placed fairy lights added a dreamlike quality to the gardens illuminated under a clear sky and half-moon. "The gardens win."

They stood, quickly making their escape through the doors to the outdoor terrace. A group of teens stood in a tight huddle at the far end of the terrace, probably up to mischief.

He grasped her hand and led her down the stone steps to a cobbled path lit with solar lanterns. "The famous rose gardens are up ahead."

They walked past a tall oak tree and followed the winding path, losing sight of the mansion behind them. Fairy lights were strung in the high tree branches, twinkling in the dense foliage as if they were stars in an inky velvet sky.

She slowed her pace, breathing in the sweet aroma of rose and jasmine. Her light jacket was draped over her chair inside, not needed in the balmy night air.

"I wish I had my camera. The gardens are divine, drenched in moonlight."

"I don't need a camera." His smile widened. "I'll commit every detail about tonight to memory."

"The wedding was lovely. The bride and groom seem very happy."

He nodded. "They are a good match." He held out his arm. "Are you ready for a moonlight stroll?"

She giggled. "You sound very serious." She hooked her arm through his.

"I have serious intentions." He traced his index finger along her cheekbone. "Let's walk."

She fell into step beside him, relieved to feel the even paving of the path underfoot. If she'd known they'd be taking a moonlight stroll, she may have worn more appropriate footwear. On the other hand, her dress needed heels to sit properly on her petite frame. Ben was over a head taller than her, despite her heels.

She sucked in a deep breath, slowing her pace. "Look at that rose."

She reached out, her fingers caressing the delicate flower. The snowy-white rose was in full bloom, not a blemish in sight in the muted moonlight. She raised her hand to her face, inhaling the fragrant perfume on her fingertips. "Exceptional."

He nodded. "I think you've found one of their award-winning roses."

"I wonder what it's called." A brass plaque was positioned on a metal stake close to the base of the bush.

She disengaged her arm from his and lifted the front of her dress, leaning forward to read the delicate script on the plaque. She wobbled on her heels, rocking back to try to maintain her balance.

He hooked his arm around her waist, providing an anchor. "You'll tumble head over heels if you're not careful."

"Thanks." Breathless, she deciphered the writing on the plaque. "'Perfection.'"

"Huh." He helped her stand upright, his arm remaining snug around her waist.

"The rose." She tilted her head back, his magnetic gaze holding her captive.

"What about the rose?"

She gulped. "Perfection. The rose is called Perfection."

He shook his head. "That can't be right. I'm holding perfection in my arms."

She lowered her lashes. "I think you're mistaken."

"No, I'm not." He traced his fingertips under her chin, the pad of his thumb lightly brushing over her closed lips. "I know perfection when I see it."

She widened her eyes, heat rising in her cheeks. His intense gaze zeroed in on her mouth, and his arm drew her closer.

She placed her hand on his shirt, the rhythmic beating of his heart pulsing through her palm. "Ben."

He lowered his head and she closed her eyes, her heart melting. His lips gently caressed hers, teasing her to welcome the new intimacy.

She groaned and parted her lips. His hand cupped her bare shoulder and he pulled her closer, his lips feathering kisses along her cheekbone before returning to her mouth.

She ran her fingers through his lustrous hair, twining his curls between her fingers.

He deepened the kiss and her mind spun into a new orbit, an avalanche of long-dormant feelings pulsing through her.

She pressed her hand against his shirt and stepped back, her breathing ragged.

"Wow." He caught her hand in his, his fingertips caressing her knuckles.

She held his magnetic gaze, reining in her unruly thoughts. "What does this mean?"

His eyes glowed in the moonlight, and he dropped a tender kiss on the back of her hand. "It means I'd like a repeat performance."

She patted her hair, glad he hadn't messed with the intricate arrangement.

He drew her close, tucking her head under his chin. "We'd better head back indoors before the bride and groom leave."

"Yes, how could we forget the wedding?" Her world had stopped and she'd forgotten everything while he held her in his strong arms.

Chapter 11

Ben draped his arm around Amy's shoulders, her creamy skin smooth under his work-roughened hands. Music blared out of the wedding-reception ballroom. "I think we're back in time."

Amy nodded. "That's a relief." She lifted the hem of her dress, pausing before climbing the stairs up to the terrace. "Do I look okay?"

He tucked a loose strand of her hair behind her ear. "You look beautiful."

"I'd better find the lipstick I stashed in my purse."

He suppressed a grin. "Your lipstick has kind of worn off."

She tilted her head back, meeting his gaze. "I must look terrible."

He shook his head, his lips curving up into a slow smile. "You look like a woman who has been thoroughly kissed."

"Ben, stop teasing me." A becoming shade of pink highlighted her delicate cheekbones.

"But it's fun." He lowered his arm around her waist to keep her balanced as she negotiated the steps. How could she even walk straight in those ridiculous heels, let alone climb stairs?

She paused at the top, moving away from him. "Do you think anyone has noticed our absence?"

He shrugged. "I couldn't care less."

"Ben." She held his gaze, her blue eyes sparkling. "Aren't you concerned people might be talking about us?"

"No, let them talk." He was proud to have her on his arm, and made no apologies for his delight in her company. It had been a long time since he'd experienced the dizzy sensations of a first kiss and he hoped he wouldn't have to wait long for a second.

She furrowed her brows. "Okay. If you're sure?"

He reached for her hand, twining his fingers through hers. "I'm sure."

They headed indoors and found empty seats at their table. The dance floor was packed with energetic guests dancing the night away to a seventies disco hit.

She let go of his hand and retrieved a small purse from her jacket pocket. "I'll be back soon, after I fix my hair and repair my makeup."

He laughed. "Don't keep me waiting too long."

"I promise I'll be quick."

He nodded. "I'll head over to the bar and order drinks. What would you like?"

"Iced water will be fine. Or a lemon soda. Whatever is easier."

"I'll bring back both."

Her smile widened. "Thanks. You're spoiling me."

"You deserve to be spoiled."

She strode toward the ladies' room, her back straight and feet steady. Amy was by far the most gorgeous and elegant woman in the room. Heads turned as she made her way across the ballroom. He clenched his fists as he noted more than one male eye lingering on her longer than he liked.

Amy disappeared into the crowd, and he joined a short line at the bar.

He collected the drinks and headed back to their table, careful not to spill the contents on either the tray or the starched white linen tablecloth. He drank half of his lemon soda and glanced around the crowded room. He didn't recognize anyone nearby, giving him an excuse to devote all his attention to Amy. His thirst quenched, he returned the tray to the bar.

"Ben, I thought that was you."

The familiar voice seeped into his mind. Why hadn't he noticed Jenny's baby sister earlier?

He turned around, giving her a bright smile. "Mary, I didn't know you were here."

"It's good to see you." She gave him a brief hug, her warm personality reminiscent of her sister. "How are the children? I haven't seen them in ages."

Guilt pricked his heart at the tiny note of censure in her voice. "They're good. Both doing well at school."

"I'm glad to hear this." Her speculative gaze rested on his flushed face. "How are you doing?"

"I'm fine."

"You're looking well."

"So are you." He shoved his hands in his pockets and glanced over Mary's shoulder. Amy should be back any minute. The last thing he'd expected to be doing tonight was introducing Amy to a member of Jenny's family.

"So, Ben, what are you up to these days?"

"The farm is keeping me busy." He paused. "We'll have to line up a lunch visit, maybe one Sunday after church?"

She narrowed her eyes. "You are bringing the children to the family Christmas gathering at Mom and Dad's next weekend?"

"Um, I guess so. I'll call your mother tomorrow." The invitation had slipped his mind.

She sighed, compassion filling eyes the same deep blue color as Jenny's. "I know it's hard, but my parents would like to see the children more often."

He nodded. If only visiting Jenny's parents' home didn't bring back so many memories. He had struggled to let go of his bitterness over her loss, but he needed to value the input her family wanted to have in his children's lives. "Is anyone else from the family here?"

"Only me. I'm dating one of the groomsmen."

"That's nice."

"I did see you earlier, but I didn't want to interrupt your time with Amy."

He let out a deep breath. "I guess that's a little awkward."

"Not really." Mary smiled. "It's time you moved on and found someone else."

"I'm glad you're okay with this."

"Life goes on, and you can't stay stuck in the past forever." She pressed her lips together, her eyes glassy. "I miss my sister heaps, but I know she'd want you and the children to be happy."

He nodded, appreciating her support.

"By the way, you two have been the talk of the wedding."

He raised an eyebrow. "Why, exactly?" Had someone seen them outside in the gardens?

"Amy oozes class and looks like a model. And you both look smitten."

"Is it that obvious?"

She nodded. "The family will be happy for you. But it may be wise to not bring Amy along to the family Christmas gathering. My mother may need a little time to get used to the idea."

"That's fine. We haven't been dating long and it could be uncomfortable."

Amy appeared at his elbow, face and hair in immaculate order. "What's uncomfortable?"

He slipped his arm around her waist. "I'll tell you on the way home."

"Okay." She tilted her head back, her wide blue eyes full of questions.

He resisted the urge to drop a kiss on her soft lips. "Have you met Mary?"

Amy lifted a brow. "I don't think so." She extended her hand to Mary. "Nice to meet you."

Mary shook her hand. "You, too. I've heard a lot about you."

"Really? Do you know my parents?"

Mary chuckled. "I think everyone knows your parents."

Ben cleared his throat and pulled Amy closer to his side. "Mary is also Jenny's younger sister."

Amy felt her smile freeze on her lips. Jenny's sister. Her gaze remained fixed on Mary's pretty face. "Oh, okay. I can see the family resemblance."

Mary nodded. "Everyone says I look like Jenny."

Ben ran his hand through his tousled hair. "That's because you both have the same eyes."

"So they say." Mary drew her brows together. "Did you know my sister?"

Amy shook her head. "I've seen photos at Ben's house."

"Amy teaches Chloe piano on Wednesday afternoons."

"Yes, Chloe is making good progress." Amy inspected her French-manicured nails, thankful he hadn't mentioned she also stayed for dinner after the lessons.

"That's great," Mary said. "Jenny always wanted Chloe to learn piano, and Declan when he's older."

Ben nodded, a distant look entering his eyes.

Amy tightened her grip on her purse, her gaze homing in on the drinks at their table. "Mary, please excuse me."

She stepped away from Ben, turning to face him. "Is my drink on the table?"

"Yes, I'll get it for you."

"No need." Mary's smile widened. "I should head back to my table. And, Ben, I look forward to seeing you and the children soon."

"Yes, that would be good."

Mary waved goodbye and walked away.

Amy lifted her chin. "Did you know she was here?"

He shook his head. "There must be nearly two hundred people here at the reception."

"True."

He cupped her elbow, steering her back to their table. "They're serving up the wedding cake. And coffee."

She wrinkled her nose. "The coffee is never any good at function venues."

He pulled out her chair. "You really are a coffee snob."

She shrugged. "I know what I like." She sat down, accepting a slice of fruitcake from a waiter circulating around their table. The seats close to them remained vacant.

She sipped her lemon soda, her throat parched. Mary's appearance tonight had unsettled her. Ben had a contemplative look shadowing his handsome face. Was he thinking about Jenny?

She tasted the cake, needing to do something to stop herself thinking about how she compared to Jenny. Mary seemed nice, but it must be hard for her to see Ben with another woman.

She placed her hand on his forearm. "Did you have a long chat with Mary?"

"Not really." He held her gaze, his eyes twinkling. "I'm a little distracted."

Her stomach sank. Was Jenny occupying his thoughts? "She does look a lot like her sister."

"Who? You mean Mary." He finished his slice of cake,

only a few crumbs remaining on his plate. "I'm usually not a fan of fruitcake, but this one is quite good."

"Yes, it's not bad. I was talking about Mary."

He reached for her hand. "It's not Mary who has distracted me."

"I know seeing Mary must remind you of Jenny."

"Hey." He twined his fingers through hers. "I only have one woman on my mind, and she is sitting right in front of me."

"Are you sure? I understand if—"

"No ifs." He swallowed hard, leaning closer to her. "Jenny was my first love, and we had a happy marriage."

Amy nodded. If only she could say the same about her own marriage.

"It took me a while, but I had to accept that she's gone and somehow move on with my life."

She blinked, moisture forming in her eyes. "I understand."

He squeezed her hand. "I'll never forget her, but I know she would want me to be happy."

"Okay." Amy had learned the hard way that it wasn't helpful to dwell on the past.

"I also have to think about what's best for my children."

"Yes, they are very important." The last thing she wanted was to see his children hurt.

"I'm sure Doug would want you to be happy, too."

She tensed, the familiar feelings of inadequacy flooding her mind. Would Doug care for her happiness now, when he'd shown little regard for her feelings while they were married? "I guess you're right."

He drained his glass. "We can only trust that God has a good plan for our future."

"Yes, life has a habit of throwing obstacles in our path."

"But they're easier to handle when we're not alone."

She closed her eyes and dipped her head, despair clutching her heart. What would he do when he learned she'd been a failure as a wife the first time around? She kept her secret close to her chest, unwilling to expose the truth about her disastrous marriage.

She looked up, nibbling her lower lip. "By the way, what was uncomfortable earlier?"

"Oh, you mean my conversation with Mary."

"Yes, the one I interrupted."

He groaned. "I forgot about an invitation to their family Christmas lunch."

"When is it?"

"Next weekend."

She lifted a brow. "Do you usually attend?"

"I haven't the last two years. Last Christmas Declan was sick." He frowned. "It was kind of a relief to have an excuse. I know that sounds lame."

She shook her head. "I would have leaped at any excuse to avoid seeing my in-laws."

"Really? That surprises me."

"It was complicated and my pedigree didn't live up to their expectations."

"Did they think they were royalty?"

She sighed. "They're an established old-money family. The type of people who would impulsively buy a million-dollar yacht because they were bored and had the spare cash lying around."

His mouth gaped open. "I had no idea."

"It's not a big deal. I'm financially comfortable and debt free. They made sure I couldn't share in the vast family fortune, not that I wanted it."

He shook his head. "I can't believe they treated you like a gold digger."

"It doesn't matter what they did or thought because that chapter of my life is thankfully over."

The music stopped and the master of ceremonies announced the impending departure of the bride and groom.

His eyes sparkled. "Yes, that chapter of your life is finished, and I'm glad you're now a part of my life."

"Me, too." She didn't want to imagine her future without Ben and his children. They had sneaked into her heart and she didn't want to do anything to jeopardize their growing relationship. Her in-laws were only a small part of the problems that had plagued her marriage to Doug.

"Are you ready to leave?"

She nodded. "It's a long drive home."

He drained his coffee cup and pushed his chair back, slipping on his jacket. He helped her into her jacket and they headed toward the dance floor near the main entrance.

The guests had formed a tunnel for the bride and groom to navigate. She stood across from Ben, their hands linked together in the air as everyone cheered the imminent departure of the newlyweds.

She held his warm gaze, his mouth curved up in a broad smile. They might reach Snowgum Creek by midnight if they had a good run home.

The bride and groom ran through their section of the tunnel and everyone lowered their arms, waving goodbye as the couple disappeared outside.

Ben moved to Amy's side, twining his fingers with hers. "You'll have to keep me awake while I drive and look out for 'roos."

She smiled. "I think I can manage that."

He led her outside and they walked to his car. "We can detour via a fast-food drive-through, if you'd like a latte for the trip home."

"Are they open this late?"

"They were when I lived here."

"Sounds good." A caffeine hit would be helpful as she kept a lookout for the kangaroos that tended to graze close to the highway. *Lord, please keep us safe as we drive back home after a wonderful evening together.*

Her skin tingled as she remembered their amazing kiss in the gardens. If only this wonderful evening could go on forever.

Chapter 12

Amy carried two mugs of hot tea into Ben's family room. The Christmas tree dominated one corner of the spacious room, colorful lights twinkling against the green foliage. A Christmas Eve carols program was on television in the background, and Ben had almost finished settling his excited children to sleep.

She curled up on the sofa, cradling her mug of tea in both hands. Luke and Rachel had left after dessert, and Amy had ducked outside to her car, bringing in her presents for Ben and the children. They were hidden at the back of the tree, ready to be opened in the morning.

Amy hummed along to a carol led by a celebrity singer on television. Tomorrow she'd see Ben at church in the morning, and return here in the evening for Christmas dinner with his family. She planned to have Christmas lunch with her family while Ben's family stayed at his farm for lunch and dinner.

Ben walked into the room, stifling a yawn. "Declan is

asleep, but Chloe is hanging in there, trying to keep her eyes open."

She smiled. "My sister and I were the same. We would sneak out of bed to see if our presents were under the tree."

"Speaking of presents, would you like to help me do some wrapping?"

"Sounds fun. Do you have many to wrap?"

He sat beside her on the sofa and sipped his tea. "Yes, I've hidden them around the house and it may take a while to retrieve them."

"Do you remember all the hiding spots?"

He narrowed his eyes. "Okay, I confess I made a list, which I wrote in code and hid in my bedroom. Chloe's curiosity means I can't stash them all on top of the shelves of the linen cupboard."

She chuckled. "My parents used to hide presents in their luggage, until they caught us investigating the contents of a suitcase."

"You were too smart for your own good."

"True. I think I drove my parents crazy."

"But they loved you to bits anyway. That's what parents do."

She squeezed the handle of her ceramic mug, her desire to experience life as a parent growing each day. He was an exceptional father, and his kids were blessed to have a devoted dad.

She finished her tea, placing the mug on the coffee table, which was usually covered in LEGO and clutter. "Will we wrap on the coffee table and watch the carols?"

He nodded. "The paper and sticky tape is on the top shelf in the linen cupboard."

"Did Chloe find it?"

"Oh, boy, was she unhappy that there were no presents to find there."

"Please tell me she didn't climb the shelves to look?"

He rubbed his hand through his hair. "She got in trouble for that, too."

"Not good." She grinned. "I'll brew a new pot of tea and find the paper while you turn the house upside down looking for their presents."

"I won't take long, I promise."

She glanced at her watch. "Do you think she's asleep?"

"I hope so. I'll have to be quiet so she won't wake."

"This present-wrapping gig is complicated."

"Last year was harder because they got new bikes for Christmas. Rachel stored them in her garage and Luke helped me assemble them."

"Did it take long?"

He shook his head. "Luke did most of the work, since he's used to building and maintaining his own bikes."

"A good plan."

He stood. "Okay, let's do it."

They split up, and she found a dozen rolls of wrapping paper, scissors and tape. How many presents did he need to wrap?

She brewed another large pot of tea, poured milk into a small ceramic jug and headed back to the living room. A number of toys were already waiting to be wrapped on the coffee table. She smiled. Operation: Christmas Presents was about to start.

She turned up the television volume and sang along to one of her all-time favorite carols. For a number of years she had struggled to muster any Christmas cheer. Last year, she had worked in Sydney over Christmas, missing her family gathering in Snowgum Creek for the fourth year in a row.

She finished wrapping a toy car, putting it aside before starting on an electronic game. Doug had insisted they stay in Sydney every Christmas to put in an appearance at his grandmother's waterfront mansion. In reality, it had been his insurance policy—a way to please his grandmother in order to maintain his inheritance when she passed. He had spent the income he earned, relying on the family trust and a potential inheritance to secure his future. A future that was never realized.

She squared her shoulders. This year, she looked forward to celebrating Christmas with her family and friends.

Ben staggered into the room, his face partially hidden by a few large boxes of LEGO. "Only one more hiding spot to go and I'll have everything in here."

She unstacked the LEGO on top. "You do know you only have two children?"

He nodded. "We have family who send me money to buy presents on their behalf. Don't worry, they aren't all from me."

"That makes sense. Did you see most of Jenny's family at the Christmas lunch?"

"Yes, it was a big gathering." He paused, his gaze reflective. "The kids had a fun time."

"And you?"

He shrugged. "It was okay. Jenny's parents are visiting us after lunch tomorrow."

"I'm glad." She returned to the coffee table, a set of books next in line. "Do you want me to wait for you to label as I wrap?"

He handed her a crumpled sheet of paper. "Here's the list."

She perused the list of names. "It's all good. I know where I'm up to on your list."

"Great. I'll be back in a minute."

She poured the tea and added milk to the strong brew.

He returned with a pink patchwork quilt. "Thanks for making a start."

"No worries." She inspected the quilt. "This is gorgeous. Did Doris make it?"

He nodded. "Chloe informed me that her current quilt is too childish."

"Really? You picked a winner with this one."

"My mother chose the design."

He wrote on the sticky labels and carried the first batch of presents to the tree. "Where did the presents at the back come from?"

She folded a large sheet of paper around the quilt. "They're from me."

"Why are they at the back?" He dropped to his knees and retrieved the presents, reading the gift tags.

"I didn't want to make a fuss."

"The kids can open their presents in the morning, but I'm saving mine until I see you tomorrow night and give you your present."

She lifted a brow. "Can I snoop tonight?"

He laughed. "I guarantee you won't find it."

"Is it in the house?"

"I'm not giving any clues." He leaped to his feet, striding across the room to join her on the floor.

She tipped her nose in the air. "Well, I'm not giving you any clues, either."

"I'm not the one dying of curiosity, remember?" He dipped his head, dropping a tender kiss on her lips. "I have other things I'm more curious about."

"Yes, but these presents won't wrap themselves. I don't want to be bleary-eyed tomorrow morning."

He grinned. "They won't take long to wrap if we work together."

"True. Let's get cracking." Christmas morning couldn't come soon enough.

Amy joined the line of parishioners waiting to enter Snowgum Creek Community Church on Christmas morning. She walked through the front doors, her gaze scanning the building that was buzzing with activity.

"Merry Christmas, Amy."

She spun around and hugged her father. "Merry Christmas. Are Mom and Bella around?"

He frowned. "Your mother is in the front row and your sister isn't here yet."

"Bella and Steve will be here." Her sister may have trouble finding a seat if she was late.

"Yes, and Ben is waving in your direction."

Ben winked and Chloe beamed a wide smile from the second-last row, where she sat next to Ben's parents.

Her father's eyes softened. "I'll see you at lunch."

"I'm looking forward to it."

She made her way to the center aisle, greeting the children and Ben's parents before slipping into the spare aisle seat beside Ben.

She met his warm gaze. "Hey."

He squeezed her hand. "Merry Christmas."

She blinked, unexpected moisture building in her eyes. "Merry Christmas."

"Did you sleep well?"

She nodded. "I was more exhausted than I'd realized." She'd called Ben at eleven-thirty, as soon as she'd arrived home, so he wouldn't worry.

"I wish I could drive you home."

"It's okay. I have my phone with me and I slow down in the 'roo danger spots." She didn't dare mention her close encounter with a kangaroo a few weeks ago, knowing he'd fret even more.

"Good. What time are you coming over this afternoon?"

"I'll text you when I leave my parents', probably around four."

"That will work well."

She lifted a brow. "Do you have plans?"

His smile widened. "You'll have to wait and see."

"Does this have something to do with my Christmas present?"

"It might." His eyes twinkled. "I promise you won't be disappointed."

Her father held a microphone at the front and welcomed the congregation to the service.

She smiled. Ben held her hand and she felt as if she belonged in his family. His parents had given her a warm welcome, unlike Doug's family. The pain of their rejection was receding, and the passing of time had helped her heal.

She stood for the opening song and Ben slipped his arm around her waist. Since the wedding a few weeks ago, they had grown closer, seeing each other most days. Ben and the children sometimes had dinner at her cottage, and she attended Ben's weekly family dinners at his parents' home. Rachel and Luke were supportive of her relationship with their older brother, and she'd become reacquainted with the elusive Caleb.

She glanced over her shoulder, spotting Bella and Steve at the back of the church. Folding chairs were set up to accommodate the overflowing congregation.

Bella mouthed *hello* and smiled, her face glowing.

She returned her sister's smile, perplexed. Bella never looked this relaxed and happy in church. Why the change? What was different about today?

The service seemed to pass quickly, and before long her father stood to give his Christmas address. The Bible readings provided the basic Christmas story, her father highlighting the importance of Jesus, God's son, being born into the world.

She closed her eyes, silently thanking God for sending His son to save her. She was under no illusion that she was good enough for God. Her guilt over her marriage failure was a firm reminder she kept tucked away in the back of her mind.

Her father talked about how Jesus had provided the way for her sins to be forgiven. Her challenge was to let go of her guilt and accept the forgiveness offered through Jesus. Could she stop punishing herself and embrace God's unconditional love?

She prayed with the congregation, her heart dwelling on the concept of forgiveness. Had she really forgiven her late husband for his failings? Or had her expectations been too high? Was it her fault that he had turned away from their marriage?

The man beside her was close to perfect. His heart was in the right place and he prioritized family and relationships. She couldn't shake the niggling guilt that her infertility had driven Doug to an early death.

She got up for the closing song, her heart full of love for Ben's family, who had welcomed her into their lives. The doubts remained, but she had to be brave and trust that Ben wouldn't intentionally hurt her.

The aisle beside her filled with people, anxious to leave and continue celebrating their Christmas Day.

She turned to Ben. "We may be waiting awhile."

He shrugged. "I don't mind because I'm with you."

His words warmed her heart, injecting her with renewed confidence. She had to start believing she deserved to have some happiness and peace in her life.

The queue finally receded, and she followed the people ahead of her to the door. Ben and his parents shook hands with her father. The children took the opportunity to bolt, chasing after their friends.

Her father's welcoming gaze rested on Ben. "You'll have to bring your children over to dinner with Amy in the next few weeks."

Ben smiled. "Sounds good."

"Dad, we'll line something up." Her gaze roamed over the lawn beside the church, spotting Bella talking with a couple of her old school friends. "I'll see you soon."

He nodded, moving on to the people behind them in line.

Chloe and Declan played tag with a few other children around the trees.

She looked up at Ben and squinted, the bright sun shining straight into her eyes. "Do you remember Bella?"

"Not really, but she's heading our way and looking very happy."

"Yes, and I'm not sure why."

He grabbed her hand and they walked along the soft lawn toward her sister and brother-in-law.

"Amy." Her sister squealed and embraced her in a big hug.

Amy stepped back, narrowing her eyes. "Bella, you're looking well."

Bella exchanged a knowing look with her husband. "Yes, and you must be Ben."

Amy performed the introductions, and Ben shook Steve's hand.

Steve raised an eyebrow. "You look familiar, mate."

"I used to service your truck at the garage in Sunny Ridge."

"Yeah, now I remember. You did a good job. What are you doing now?"

"Apple orchards."

"A tough business. Do you still service cars?"

"Only for family and friends. The farm and my kids keep me busy."

Bella glanced at Ben's fingers linked with hers. "I think we fall into that category."

Amy's face flushed and she lowered her lashes.

"Sure," Ben said. "Give me a call if you need some work done."

"We will." Bella's smile widened. "And we have an announcement."

Amy lifted a brow. "I assume it's good news."

"I'm pregnant."

Amy's stomach lurched, as if she had been punched hard in the solar plexus. Pregnant. The words permeated her mind. Her sister was having a baby.

"Congratulations." She hugged her sister, squeezing her eyes shut. She could hold it together and not ruin her sister's special moment.

"I was planning to tell you at lunch, but I couldn't keep it a secret any longer."

Amy nodded, pressing her lips together.

Bella snuggled closer to Steve, a protective hand resting on her flat stomach. "I'm sure Mom and Dad will be excited to hear they will soon be grandparents."

Ben's smile froze, concern filling his heart. Amy's face had paled and she dug her fingernails into the palm of his hand.

He turned to Bella and Steve. "Congratulations."

"Thanks." Bella giggled. "We're still getting used to the idea and I'm so excited."

He nodded. "It's great news."

Amy lifted her gaze, her smile not quite making it to her eyes. "I should probably get going. I'd like to see Chloe and Declan before I leave."

"Sure," Bella said. "We'll see you soon at Mom and Dad's for lunch."

Amy strode away from her sister at top speed.

Ben jogged to keep up with her. "Amy, we need to talk."

She slowed her pace and turned to him, her eyes brimming with unshed tears. "How could she do that to me?"

"What?"

She raked her hands through her hair, twisting the ends around her fingers. "Rub her good news in my face."

"I don't think that was her intention."

She shook her head. "She always has to outdo me in everything, and this is no different."

"Hey." He tipped her chin up, catching her tempestuous gaze. "I think you may be reading too much into this. Does Bella know about your fertility issues?"

"Sort of."

He raised an eyebrow. "What haven't you told her?"

"She doesn't know a lot about my marriage." She stepped back, crossing her arms over her chest. "She can be so insensitive."

He inhaled a calming breath, counting to three before speaking. "I think it would help to try and look at the situation from her perspective."

Amy's lower lip trembled. "She's glowing with happiness."

"She enjoyed sharing her special news with her sister. She told you before she told your parents. Doesn't that count for something?"

She pressed her fingertips on her eyelids. "I don't know. I always thought I'd be the first daughter to provide my parents with grandchildren."

"It's okay." He drew her into his arms, stroking her hair. "Bella is really excited and she wants to share her joy with you."

"I guess so." A tear slipped out from under her lashes.

"You do realize this means you'll become an aunt next year."

She grunted.

"And you'll make a wonderful aunt for your little nephew or niece." He wiped away another tear that had escaped down her cheek.

A new vulnerability clouded her eyes. "It just hurts so much."

"I know." He continued stroking her hair, and her body started to relax in his arms.

"I'm sorry to be blubbering like a baby."

"It's okay. For what it's worth, I still remember how excited I was when I learned Jenny was pregnant with Chloe."

"I'm happy for Bella and Steve." She sniffed. "It's just really hard when she's experiencing what I always wanted and can't have."

"It will get easier, once you get used to the idea and the initial shock has worn off. Why don't we find the kids? They brought a couple of presents in the car to show you."

"Really?" Her face brightened.

He nodded. "You're becoming an important part of their lives." His children adored Amy. She was a mother figure to them, whether she realized it or not.

He blew out a stream of air, the full impact of her emotional angst registering in his mind. He wished he could do something to make her feel better and remove the frown lines marring her smooth forehead.

Chapter 13

Ben lounged back in a padded wicker chair on his veranda, his feet resting on the wooden railing. Luke sat beside him, his attention focused on his new smartphone.

"My kids are glad you're not working Christmas Day."

Luke nodded. "I'm on call at the hospital later."

"What are you doing?"

"Texting a friend."

He raised an eyebrow. "A female friend, by any chance?"

"Yes, a friend who happens to be female."

Ben laughed. "Another one of your groupies. There will come a time when women will stop fawning over you."

"It's not like that."

He slapped his brother on the back. "They're all lining up to marry the new doctor in town."

"Speaking of marriage, are we going to have a wedding in the family next year?"

"We need to harvest a bumper apple crop before I can answer that question."

Luke frowned. "Have things gotten worse?"

Ben rubbed his hand over his face, fatigue from his financial stress drawing his brows together. "A few unexpected expenses have cropped up. I may need to chase a couple more jobs as a mechanic to tide us over."

"I can help you out if you get stuck."

"No, you need your money for that big house you're planning to build. Are the building plans approved?"

"Not yet, but I'm hopeful I'll get the green light early next year."

Ben grinned. "Your popularity with the ladies is going to explode when they realize you're building the mansion on the hill."

He shrugged. "I'm too busy working to pay attention to these things."

"That's what I used to say." He glanced at his watch. "Amy should be here any minute. Can you watch the kids for an hour or so?"

"Sure. Are you going somewhere?"

"No, but I have a surprise planned."

"Okay. I've seen Declan riding around, but where's Chloe?"

"Somewhere on the farm with Rachel and Caleb. They were talking about riding the motorbikes."

Luke glanced up, his eyes widening. "You trust Chloe on the back of a bike with our brother?"

"No, but I trust our sister." He could depend on Rachel to ensure that Chloe stayed out of mischief.

"True." Luke sat up straighter in his seat. "Amy's here."

"Thanks. I'll see you later." Ben leaped out of his seat and headed over to Amy's usual parking spot.

He opened her car door and she stepped out, her floral dress swirling around her knees.

She gave him a brilliant smile. "Did you have a nice lunch?"

"Yes, and you?"

"It went surprisingly well. I think the baby news will bring my sister and parents closer together."

"I'm glad." He drew her into his arms. "And you're okay?"

She nodded. "You were right."

He lowered his head, his lips feathering a gentle kiss over her lips. "I can finally kiss you without little eyes watching."

She giggled. "Have you opened your present from me?"

"Not yet." He draped his arm around her shoulders. "We can go inside and I'll open it before I show you my surprise."

She fell into step beside him and they made their way to the family room. The square-shaped gift had pride of place in front of the Christmas tree.

He pointed to a pile of presents on one side of the tree. "Those are for you to open tonight. From my family."

"I have their presents in the car." She picked up his gift and handed it to him. "I hope you like it."

He smiled, holding her warm gaze. "I'm sure I will." He ripped open the gold paper, revealing a coffeemaker and a large bag of ground coffee.

He laughed. "Are you sure you didn't buy yourself a present?"

"You don't like it?"

"Of course I do." He dropped a kiss on her full lips. "You have convinced me of the benefits of good coffee."

Her eyes sparkled. "I'll make a pot for everyone later."

"Sounds great." He glanced at the delicate sandals encasing her petite feet. "Are your walking boots still out in the back room?"

"They're in my car."

"Good."

She lifted a brow. "Ben, what do you have planned?"

"I'll tell you after you change into more appropriate footwear." He looked forward to her reaction when she found her Christmas present from him.

Amy perched on the edge of a chair on the veranda and tied her shoelaces. She was thankful she'd kept a clean pair of socks in the car with her boots. She furrowed her brow. The boots didn't look right with her knee-length summer dress, but they'd give her some protection if she happened to come across a snake.

Ben held out his hand. "Ready, pretty lady?"

She stood. "Where are we going?"

"I thought we could take a walk in the orchards."

"Okay." It would do her good to walk off the extra calories from lunch.

They headed along a wide track separating two sections of the orchard. A swishing sound in the grass under a tree caught her attention.

She gripped his hand. "What was that?"

"Probably a snake. I've seen a few around, which is why the kids aren't allowed to wander through the orchards without an adult."

She frowned. "Are they listening?"

"Chloe is, after she found a brown snake curled up near the shed before lunch."

Amy gasped. "Was she scared?"

"Our neighbors could have heard her scream, and she is now shadowing her auntie Rachel."

"Poor Chloe."

"But I'm more concerned about Declan."

"Why? Has he ignored your wishes?"

"He has no fear."

She grinned. "He's a boy."

"And he's still riding his bike everywhere." He sighed. "I've tried to convince him to stay near the house."

She shivered, leaning in closer to his arm. If she spotted even one snake, he'd have to carry her back to the house.

They climbed the rise of the hill, a spectacular view of the valleys and pine forests beyond the apple orchards stealing her breath. She inhaled the fresh air from the nearby mountains, marveling at the natural beauty of God's creation.

He hugged her close to his side, his gaze tender. "One day I'll show you a sunset from up here."

"I imagine they are incredible."

He led her down a row of apple trees, heavy with fruit ripening on the branches.

She paused, running her thumb over a flawless red apple. "Your crop is looking good."

"I hope it stays that way." His terse voice exuded tension.

"Are you worried something will go wrong?"

"Farmers always worry about their crops."

A large part of the orchard was covered in white hail netting, and scare guns blasted at regular intervals to deter the birds. The cockatoos were the worst offenders, leaving a trail of destruction in their wake.

"I'll pray you'll harvest a bumper crop."

He smiled, his eyes crinkling in the corners. "Thanks."

They walked in companionable silence, eventually leaving the orchards and heading into the large garden toward the front of the house. A white painted gazebo was situated on the far side, pink climbing roses adding a touch of color.

She stepped into the gazebo. A three-foot-tall potted white rosebush sat in the center, Christmas paper wrapped around the base.

She gasped. "Ben, it's beautiful." She leaned forward and inhaled the fragrant perfume. "The tiny buds are exquisite."

His smile widened. "I searched everywhere to find a bush similar to the one you liked at the wedding."

"It's the perfect present. Thank you." She stood on her tiptoes, placing her lips against his for a brief kiss.

He wrapped his arm around her waist. "Merry Christmas, sweetheart."

She sighed, her head resting against his hard chest, feeling safe and secure in his embrace. She had fallen head over heels in love with this handsome man, and she didn't want this marvelous Christmas Day to end.

Ben picked up the potted rosebush and strolled back toward the house. Amy walked close by his side, and the late-afternoon sun blasted his face. A hint of a breeze whistled through the treetops, cooling his bare forearms.

Amy's smile broadened, her blue eyes twinkling in the golden light. "I'm going to find a sunny position on my back deck for the rosebush."

"A good idea."

Declan ran toward them, hauling a cricket bat through the grass. "Amy, look at my new bat."

Ben frowned. "You're going to ruin it if you drag it along the ground."

His son pouted. "No, I won't."

Amy crouched down, checking out the bat. "Wow. You'll soon be hitting lots of sixes."

"Uncle Caleb gave it to me for Christmas."

She nodded. "It's a great present and the right size for you."

Declan stood tall, puffing out his chest. "Will you play cricket with me?"

Ben ruffled his son's hair. "Not today. Amy's not dressed for cricket."

She stood. "I'll be back tomorrow morning and we can all have a bash in the yard."

Ben smiled. "If you're lucky, you might be able to talk your uncles into playing with you before dinner."

"I'll go look for Uncle Caleb. Is he in the orchards?"

"Not sure, but please remember to watch out for snakes."

Declan scrunched his nose. "You worry too much."

"It's my job."

Declan ignored his comment and ran away, holding his brand-new bat high off the ground.

Amy continued walking beside Ben. "Are your parents due back soon?"

He nodded. "They're catching up with friends this afternoon."

"My parents have organized dinner with a few people who are on their own for Christmas. Now that they're getting older, my folks are finding it too hard to put on a big lunch straight after the morning service."

"It's good that they can take care of those who don't have family nearby."

"Yes." She tucked a few loose locks of hair behind her ears. "It's not fun being on your own on Christmas Day."

He reached the veranda and placed the pot on the top step. He held her gentle gaze, a faraway look shadowing her eyes. "Has that happened to you?"

She nodded, lowering her lashes.

"When?"

"Last year. My boss couldn't approve my leave request and I ended up working a double shift."

"That's terrible."

She stared at the steps. "Someone has to work on Christmas Day in our hospitals."

"True, but it's hard when you're living away from your family."

"It's another reason I moved back."

He tipped up her chin, his thumb tracing a path along her cheekbone "Do you feel settled in Snowgum Creek?"

She nodded. "This is home, and my parents plan to stay here after Dad retires in a couple of years."

His heart warmed, hope for a bright future gaining momentum in his mind. If his plans for harvesting a bumper apple crop fell into place, he could take steps to make his relationship with Amy more permanent.

Amy sat between Chloe and Declan at the dining-room table, helping them to build their new LEGO creations. Declan's plane was almost finished, but Chloe's pink café needed a fair bit of work.

Ben appeared in the doorway, holding two bowls of ice cream. "Chloe, Declan, do you have room for ice cream?"

Declan nodded, his attention focused on his plane.

Chloe smiled. "Thanks, Dad."

Amy cleared a space for the bowls in front of the children. "Do you want any help with dessert?"

He shook his head. "Mom and Dad are cleaning up the kitchen with Rachel. Can I tempt you with apple pie and ice cream?"

"Made with your apples?"

"Of course." He grinned. "I only use the best."

"Well, that's an offer I can't refuse," she said, and Ben left to get the desserts.

Luke had been called to the hospital halfway through dinner, and Caleb had left soon after to drive back to his home in Sunny Ridge. Ben believed Caleb had made arrangements to meet his new girlfriend tonight.

Ben's family had exchanged presents with Amy before dinner, and she'd been touched by the effort they had put in to make her feel welcome.

Rachel returned to the dining room. "Wow. The LEGO building is going well."

"Amy is the best at helping," Declan said.

Chloe frowned. "You've been hogging her attention. I want Amy to help me now, instead of you."

Declan glared at his sister. "You're older and don't need much help."

"Hey," Rachel said. "Can we please not fight over Amy at the table?"

"Yes," Ben said, entering the room with his parents in tow. "Or there will be no ice cream for the rest of the week."

Chloe scrunched her nose and finished her dessert. "I want to read one of my new books tonight."

Ben's mother slipped into a spare seat beside Chloe. "I'm sure you'll choose a good one."

Ben placed a bowl of freshly baked apple pie and ice cream in front of Amy.

She inhaled the delectable aroma of apple and cinnamon. "Mmm, this looks great. Thank you."

He winked. "Enjoy."

She tasted a mouthful of pie, the beautifully cooked apples and pastry melting in her mouth.

Ben's father cleared his throat. "Amy, we're really glad you could join us tonight."

Her eyes misted. "I've enjoyed spending Christmas night with you all."

Chloe placed her hand on Amy's arm. "Can I read to you tonight?"

Her gaze connected with Ben's, and he nodded his approval. "Of course," Amy said. "After I've finished your daddy's delicious pie."

She swallowed her last mouthful of pie, excused herself from the table and followed Chloe to her bedroom. The new pink quilt covered Chloe's bed.

"I usually read before I clean my teeth and get changed into my pajamas."

"No worries."

"But I like to do my prayers first, before I'm too tired to think of what to say."

Amy smiled. "A good idea." She sat on the bed beside Chloe. "Do you say your prayers aloud?"

Chloe nodded, closing her eyes and resting her hand on Amy's knee. "Dear God, thank You for the best Christmas Day ever. My presents were excellent and I had so much fun riding the motorbike with Uncle Caleb."

Amy inhaled a sharp breath. Did Ben know that Caleb had taken his daughter for a ride?

"And, God, thank You for Amy. You haven't answered my prayer for a new mommy yet, but Amy is doing a good job while I wait."

Amy dug her teeth into her lower lip, tears threatening to flow from under her closed eyelids. Chloe had touched a place deep inside her that needed healing. Her kind words were a soothing balm.

"And thank You for Daddy. I like how he is happy and smiles more often." The little girl sighed. "I missed his smile. Amen."

Chloe opened her eyes. "Did I pray the right way?"

Amy nodded, her words choking in her throat. "You did great. Auntie Rachel has taught you well."

Chloe took her time choosing something to read, poring over the back-cover information on each of her new books.

Amy blinked away a few tears. This precious girl had given her hope. Could she be the answer to Chloe's prayers? Did Ben have marriage on his mind? Her confidence grew. Had God answered her prayers and given her a family to love?

Chapter 14

Amy wiped the back of her hand over her brow, beads of sweat sliding over her skin. Her wide-brimmed hat protected her face from the harsh January sun. She had slathered sunscreen over her bare arms and legs, although it felt as though it was melting off her skin in the summer heat.

Declan waited in front of a plastic trash bin, cricket bat in hand. Chloe stood behind the bin, hands on her hips. Lily dropped a dirty tennis ball, covered in dog slobber, at Amy's feet.

She patted Lily's head. "Good girl. You're an excellent fielder."

Lily barked, her tail swinging rapidly behind her.

"Hurry up, Amy. I want to get Declan out and have a turn at batting."

Declan poked his tongue out at his sister. "I'm going to be batting for ages, like the Aussies on television."

Chloe glared at her brother. "Amy will bowl you out."

"I'll try." Amy picked up the slimy ball, wrinkling her

nose. Her hands would need a thorough wash when they finished the game.

"Amy, I'm ready." Declan stood in front of the bin, bat raised and ready to belt another ball into the yard for Lily to fetch.

Amy bowled an underarm delivery, doing her best to aim for the bin. The ball bounced wide and Declan smashed it over her head.

Lily raced across the grass and leaped into the air, catching the ball before it bounced.

"Yes!" Chloe jumped up and down. "Go, Lily."

Ben clapped from the veranda, a wide grin covering his face. "This is entertaining."

Amy smiled. "Would you like a turn at bowling?"

He shook his head, walking across the lawn toward her.

Lily dropped the ball at her feet, panting hard. "Good work, Lily."

Chloe sank to her knees and gave Lily a big hug. "You're the best dog, and now it's my turn to bat."

Declan pouted. "It's not fair."

"Come on, Declan," Ben said. "Remember how we talked about good sportsmanship."

"But I wanted to bat longer—"

"No buts. Anyway, no one will be batting for a while because a storm is brewing."

Amy gazed at the clear blue sky. "I can't see anything."

Ben pointed to a small mass of clouds building on the horizon. "Over there."

"Do you think it's heading our way?"

He frowned. "I'm not taking any chances and I need to check the orchards. Where are your car keys?"

"On the kitchen counter with my purse."

"I'll move your car into the shed."

"Thanks." She'd forgotten her car was outside and unprotected from the weather.

"Can you please close up the house and keep the kids inside? And Lily—she goes ballistic if she's outside during a storm."

"Okay."

His gaze softened. "I'll be back as soon as I can, and I appreciate you watching the kids during your holidays."

"No problem. It's been fun."

He winked. "See you soon."

She helped the children clean up the yard. They packed away the cricket equipment and other toys before heading over to the house with Lily. Chloe ran ahead and Declan paused on the veranda.

"Can I watch the cricket on TV?" he asked.

"Not if a storm is coming and we might lose power or have lightning strikes close by."

His shoulders sank. "I guess I can play with my cars."

"There'll be time to watch the cricket later. Do you remember your father saying you can't have the television on all day?"

He narrowed his eyes. "Your memory is too good."

She chuckled. "Come on, let's go inside. I need to close up the house in case the storm hits us."

Declan walked ahead to the bathroom, shoulders slouched.

She sighed. One day, she'd like to take Declan to see his cricket heroes play live in either Sydney or Melbourne.

She washed her hands, glad to see Chloe and Declan had already cleaned up ahead of her. They were good kids, well behaved and a pleasure to watch.

The bathroom window squeaked as she pulled it shut. Then she methodically worked her way around the house, shutting all the external doors and windows.

She reached Ben's closed bedroom door, her hand resting on the door handle. She felt like an intruder in his private space, but she was certain his window had been left open.

She twisted the handle and pushed the door open, entering his room. Ben's masculine scent filled her nostrils and her gaze took in his immaculate room, nothing out of place. A blue-toned quilt was draped over the king-size bed that dominated the spacious room. A decent-sized walk-in wardrobe was located opposite the bed, right next to a half-open sliding door that partially concealed a bathroom.

What would Ben think of her messy bedroom? She had clothes draped everywhere and shoes lying around. Her wardrobe was overflowing, and she needed to buy another storage solution to accommodate her extensive clothing-and-shoe collection.

She strode across the room and closed the window behind a billowing curtain. The sky outside had darkened, heralding the imminent arrival of the storm.

She hurried back to the hall and pulled the door shut behind her. Next stop was the laundry.

"Amy, I need help." Chloe's voice carried down the hall from the kitchen.

"What's wrong?"

"I can't get the lid off the honey jar."

"Okay, I'm coming." She walked into the kitchen.

Chloe sat on a stool at the kitchen island, an open loaf of bread beside her plate. "The lid is stuck."

Amy held the glass jar, wrenching the lid off on her second attempt. "Here you go."

Declan ran into the kitchen, followed by Lily.

Chloe pointed to the door. "Lily, out."

Lily dropped her tail and meandered out of the kitchen.

Declan smiled. "Amy, can you please make me a sandwich?"

"Sure." Lily dropped to the floor just outside the kitchen entrance, her eyes downcast. Ignoring the dog, Amy put together a sandwich for Declan. She closed the kitchen window. The laundry window was the last one she needed to check.

"Amy, I'm thirsty," Declan said. "Can I please have some apple juice?"

"Sure." She found two plastic cups and poured juice for the children.

Declan scooted up on a stool and sat beside Chloe. They munched on their sandwiches and drank their juice.

Amy filled the electric kettle with water before switching it on. A nice cup of tea was what she needed.

An enormous bang sounded through the kitchen. Startled, she jumped, the loud thunder grating her nerves. Lily barked, her paws tapping on the wooden floorboards as she ran along the hall.

Chloe whimpered. "I've spilled my juice."

"It's okay." Amy found a cloth and cleaned up the small puddle of juice on the island in front of Chloe.

Another clap of thunder echoed through the room, followed by silence.

Declan cocked his head to the side. "Where's Lily?"

She lifted a brow. "She must be somewhere in the house."

"But she always barks after the thunder."

She gasped. "Oh, no, the laundry." She ran from the kitchen, Declan and Chloe hot on her heels. She entered the laundry, her stomach sinking. The external door was flung open, blowing in the wind.

Declan's eyes widened. "Lily has escaped. I have to find her."

"Declan, wait."

"No." He ran onto the veranda and down the steps to the lawn.

She turned to Chloe. "Promise me you'll wait here while I catch your brother and Lily."

Chloe nodded, tears brimming in her eyes. "I promise."

Amy hugged Chloe before racing outside into the wild weather. Fortunately, Declan's orange T-shirt was easy to spot as he headed toward the orchard.

"Declan, stop," she shouted. Her chest burned and she panted, slowing to suck in more air. Large drops of rain pelted her face. She had to bring him back to the house before the hailstorm hit.

Ben revved the motorbike engine, raindrops splattering on his face. He rode along the boundary fence of the far orchard at the back of the property, almost ready to return to the house. He had secured the hail netting, doing everything possible to protect his crop from the coming storm.

His chest tightened. The apples were only weeks away from being ready to pick. Early indications from the markets suggested that the prices were looking good this year. And he had a large crop of high-grade apples. If he could harvest the whole orchard at a good price, the profit would provide him with a much-needed financial buffer for the coming year.

He swung the bike around a tight corner, powering up the hill and back toward the house. The wind whipped through his hair and rain pelted his back. He braced his body, hoping he could make it back to the house before the hail started to fall.

If hail wiped out the uncovered sections of the orchard, he'd have another hard year of financial stress to manage. He gripped the bike handles, adrenaline racing through his limbs. This couldn't be happening. He was so close to harvesting the crop. *Please, Lord, spare us from the hail. We need a good-quality crop to harvest at a decent price.*

His plans to propose marriage to Amy were on shaky ground. She had become an important part of his life. He loved her and couldn't imagine her not being in his life. His stomach sank. How could he provide for Amy, when he could barely afford to support himself and the children?

Amy had lived a life of luxury in Sydney. How could he compete with her former life? She deserved a husband who could love and cherish her in every way. If hail struck the orchard, his hope of a future with Amy would be bleak.

Ben caught a flash of orange in his peripheral vision. Declan? No, he must be mistaken. Declan should be inside with Amy and Chloe.

An image of Declan wearing his orange T-shirt and holding his cricket bat formed in his mind. What was his son doing, running around outside in a hailstorm?

His mouth drawn into a thin line, Ben slowed the bike and changed direction. He had to make sure Declan took shelter from the storm. Why had Amy let him leave the house, when he had specifically asked her to keep the children indoors?

He clenched his jaw, the constant downpour soaking his T-shirt and pounding harder against his face. He cringed. Declan ran near the edge of the orchard, and it looked as though Amy was outside chasing him. Were they crazy? Why couldn't they both listen to him and follow instructions? Now they were all going to get caught in the hailstorm.

Amy slowed her pace, her breathing shallow. "Declan, come back!"

He ignored her, running farther from the house along the edge of the orchard and looking down each row.

Where was Lily? Amy paused at the edge of the lawn, certain she could hear barking from the direction of the house. The rain cooled her sweaty skin and she shivered. Her navy blue T-shirt was damp from the rain. She shook her head, rainwater flying off her ponytail.

"Declan, stop."

He didn't slow or turn around. Why couldn't he hear her shouting? She bent forward, resting her hands on her knees as she tried to catch her breath. Declan could outrun her way too easily, even without a head start.

She sucked in a deep breath and bolted after Declan. He had wandered deeper into the orchards. She waited at the top of a row and waved him back. "Declan."

He spun around. "Where's Lily?"

"I thought I heard her barking near the house." She stood at the edge of the orchard, hands on her hips. "We need to go back before the hail starts."

"But I have to find Lily."

Lightning lit up the orchard, the iridescent white light giving the apple trees an eerie glow.

"Declan, you must come back inside with me *now*."

A motor revved in the distance. Ben. Her pulse raced even faster. He'd go berserk if he found Declan outside.

Declan stood still, waving his hands in the air. "Lily, where are you?"

"We've run out of time. I can hear your father's bike, and if he finds you out here…"

His eyes widened as he walked toward her. "I can't leave Lily out here all alone."

"But we don't even know if she's in the orchard." Lily could be anywhere. *Lord, please help us find Lily ASAP.*

A clap of thunder echoed around them, and tree branches rocked in the wind. Panic started to rise in her chest.

The rain eased and Declan joined her at the top of the row.

"Amy, I'm scared for Lily."

"I know." Guilt weighed heavily in her heart. If she had remembered to make sure the laundry door was shut, they wouldn't be in this predicament.

"Do you really think she is back at the house?"

She nodded, swiping strands of wet hair off her face. "She's a smart dog and she is probably sheltering from the rain back at the house."

"I don't know."

She placed a comforting hand on his shoulder. "Once we return to the house, we can work out a plan."

"Dad can whistle and she usually comes home."

The low roar of a motorbike filled the orchard. She turned around to find Ben coming toward them.

He drew the bike to a sliding stop a few feet behind them, the engine idling. "What are you two doing out here?"

"Lily is missing."

"What?" His eyes narrowed. "How did that happen?"

Amy pressed her lips together. "It's my fault. I didn't realize the laundry door was open."

Ben ran his hand through his damp hair. "Okay, we have a lull before the hail hits."

"Hail." Declan's eyes became as wide as saucers.

"Yes, hail, which is why you should be inside." He looked around. "Where's Chloe?"

She sighed. "I made her promise to stay on the veranda and wait for us."

"Daddy, I'm sorry I ran off." Declan's lower lip trembled. "I'm really scared for Lily."

"I know you are, son." His voice softened. "I need to put the bike away. Amy, can you walk with Declan back to the house?"

She nodded.

"If Lily isn't with Chloe, I'll whistle her back."

Declan's face brightened. "Will Lily come home when you whistle?"

"I hope so. She may be hiding near the house anyway."

Amy let out a deep breath, reaching for Declan's hand. "We need to get moving."

"See you at the house." Ben revved the engine and rode past them toward the drive leading to the sheds behind the house.

Declan's grip tightened on her hand. "Daddy is really mad at me."

"It's my fault, as well." She furrowed her brow. "Lily would still be inside if I'd checked the laundry door."

"Last time Lily ran away during a storm, she didn't come home for hours."

"I'm sure Lily is fine. She may even be with Chloe now." Poor Chloe, left alone on the veranda while the storm grew wilder. Amy was thankful Chloe was old enough to understand the importance of staying at the house.

They retraced their steps back toward the house. The sky grew darker and the air stilled. Goose bumps rose along her arms and her chest constricted. Chloe stood alone on the veranda and waved when she caught sight of them.

Amy kept Declan beside her on the track, less than a hundred yards from shelter. They could take a shortcut across the lawn, but the grass looked slippery after the earlier rainfall.

Small drops of rain bounced off her face. She quickened her pace to avoid the next downpour, and Declan half jogged to keep up with her.

Ben appeared beside Chloe, and a low whistle sounded through the yard. He whistled a second time, and a bark broke the silence.

Lily sped across the lawn and ran up the steps to the veranda. Chloe grabbed hold of Lily's collar.

"Lily." Declan tore his hand from Amy's grip and raced onto the lawn.

She walked behind Declan, spotting a streak of yellow moving in the grass in front of him.

"Declan, stop!" She froze, her mouth gaping open. A snake was on the move less than twenty feet ahead of her.

Chapter 15

Amy dug her fingernails into her palms, fear clutching her heart.

Declan kept running and the tiger snake reared up a few feet off the ground.

Ben leaped over the veranda railing, terror filling his eyes. "Declan, run back to Amy."

Chloe screamed and Declan glanced sideways, the momentum of his body taking him into the snake's path.

Thunder shattered the sky and the snake disappeared from sight.

Declan shrieked, his right leg seeming to go limp as he reached his father.

"No!" Amy raced back to the drive and skirted around the lawn. Icy balls of hail started to fall from the sky and she pumped her legs hard, adrenaline shooting through her body.

Ben carried Declan back to the veranda. Tears rolled down Declan's face. She pulled her phone out of her pocket and pressed the emergency number on her speed dial.

Ben held Declan in his arms. Declan's right leg revealed puncture marks above his ankle.

She caught Ben's wide-eyed gaze. "Tiger snake?"

"Yep." He lowered his body into a chair, his attention focused on calming his son.

"Don't move him. I'll get the compression bandage." She turned to Chloe. "Can you take Lily inside, call Uncle Luke and bring the phone to me?"

Chloe nodded. She held Lily's collar as she raced inside.

Amy followed and located the first-aid kit in the laundry cupboard. She gave the necessary information to the emergency operator, and an ambulance was dispatched. Hail pummeled the roof, sounding like bullets.

Chloe passed the house phone to her, and Amy answered Luke's questions. Juggling the first-aid kit in one hand, she rushed back to the veranda. She closed the door to prevent Lily from following her and Chloe outside.

Declan's eyes were squeezed shut, the intense pain evident on his pale face.

"Definitely a tiger snake?" Luke asked.

"Yes. Are you nearby?"

"Five minutes away and I have antivenin with me."

"Good, you may beat the ambulance."

She disconnected the call, handing the phone back to Chloe. "An ambulance and Luke are on their way."

Ben nodded. "Thanks."

She held Declan's wrist, checking his pulse. "Is his breathing normal?"

"I think so."

"Keep him as still as you can while I apply the bandage."

She rummaged through the first-aid kit, finding the appropriate pressure bandage. "Okay, Declan, I need you to be brave and try to stay calm. The bandage will help stop the venom from leaving your leg."

She wrapped the bandage around his lower leg, her fingers moving on autopilot as her mind reeled in shock.

Luke's Jeep screeched to a halt on the drive. He ran toward them, his doctor's bag bouncing against his leg. The lawn was a sea of white ice, the hailstones starting to melt as sunshine broke through the cloud cover.

"How long since the bite?" Luke asked.

"Less than ten minutes," she said.

Luke ripped his bag open and prepared a syringe full of antivenin. He turned to his nephew. "This may hurt a bit, but it will make you better and kill the poison."

Declan bit his lower lip, fresh tears flowing down his face.

Amy stepped back and let Luke take over, knowing she had done everything in her power to help Declan.

Chloe threw her arms around Amy's waist, sobs racking her small body. An ambulance siren blared through the still air. Amy held Chloe close, stroking her hair. *Lord, please help Declan's body fight the poison and recover quickly from the bite.*

Ben held his son's limp body in his arms. Declan's face was contorted in a grimace, the pain from the snakebite and antivenin injection battering his body. *Lord, thank You for bringing Luke here so fast.*

Amy stood back, holding his daughter close to her side. Chloe had been so brave. Amy's eyes were closed, a couple of tears sneaking out from between her lashes.

Luke packed up his medical bag, kneeling on the wooden veranda. "He's going to be okay."

"Thank you." He met his brother's concerned gaze. "If you hadn't been close by…"

The ambulance pulled up the drive, and two paramedics headed in their direction.

Luke stood. "They got here fast." He greeted the two

men and gave them an update on Declan's condition as they examined their patient.

The older paramedic smiled. "You're a lucky boy, having your uncle nearby at a time like this."

Declan's eyelids fluttered open and he attempted to smile.

"And we need to take you to the hospital." The paramedic turned to Ben. "Has he ridden in an ambulance before?"

Ben shook his head, his gaze remaining focused on Declan. "This will be a new adventure for all of us."

The younger paramedic carried a stretcher from the ambulance and placed it beside Declan.

Chloe's face lit up. "Daddy, can I come, too?"

"Not this time, sweetheart."

Luke grabbed hold of his niece's hand, his voice gentle. "You can follow with me and Amy."

Chloe pouted and Luke gave her a brief hug. "Your father needs to go with your brother, but I'll take care of you."

The paramedics lifted Declan onto the stretcher, keeping his leg immobilized. Ben stood, stretching out his back as he followed them to the ambulance.

Luke walked beside him with Chloe. "We won't be far behind you."

He frowned. "Can you find my wallet? I left it somewhere in my room."

"Sure, and I'll grab a spare change of clothes for both of you. They may keep Declan in the hospital overnight."

"Thanks." Hail crunched under his shoes, and he glanced over at the orchards. Specks of white ice were visible on the ground between the trees. He let out a big sigh, defeated. His beautiful apples were ruined.

Amy stood alone on the veranda, her arms wrapped around her body and her face stricken.

He turned to Luke. "Can you make sure Amy's okay?"

"No problem. Her quick action has helped save Declan's life."

Ben nodded, his attention returning to his orchards. All that work for nothing. Five minutes of hail and the uncovered portion of his crop was destroyed.

He followed Declan into the back of the ambulance, taking a seat beside one of the paramedics. He held Declan's hand, his gaze intent on his son's face as the paramedics hooked up equipment around him. *Lord, thank You that Declan is safe.*

Amy leaned her arms on the wooden veranda railing. Sunlight beamed on hailstones that looked like crystals scattered on the lawn. The ambulance drove away and Luke returned with Chloe.

He met her eyes. "How are you doing?"

"All right."

His gaze softened. "Your quick action saved his life."

"I guess so." Declan's life wouldn't have been in danger if she hadn't messed up by forgetting to check the door.

Chloe gripped her uncle's hand, her lower lip trembling. "I'm scared for Declan."

"He'll be fine," Luke said. "The hospital staff will monitor him and he'll be home soon."

Amy sighed. "What do you need me to do?"

"We need to go to the hospital. Is your car around somewhere?"

"Ben parked it under cover in the shed."

She walked inside with Luke and Chloe. Lily barked and danced around them as they made their way to the kitchen.

Chloe patted Lily. "Can she go outside now?"

"She sure can, now the storm has passed." She fished her car keys off the kitchen counter and handed them to Luke.

"I'll let Lily out soon." He drew his brows together. "Do you have a change of clothes?"

"In my car." She'd learned to keep spare clothes in the car during her frequent visits to the farm.

"I'll lock up and bring your car around to the drive." He shoved her car keys in his pocket. "If you and Chloe can pack a bag for Declan, I'll find the stuff that Ben wants."

"No problem."

"I have to go to the clinic after I stop in and see Declan." He ran his hand through his hair. "I've already pushed back my afternoon appointments."

She nodded. He'd be busy at the clinic because she was on annual leave.

"Uncle Luke, can I go in your car?"

He smiled. "Sure."

"And sit in the front?"

"Don't push your luck, kiddo." He turned to Amy. "Are you okay to drive?"

"Yep."

"I'll call my parents and get them to meet us at the hospital."

"Sounds like a good plan."

Chloe smiled. "I'll find his favorite cars."

"Great idea," Amy said. "I'm sure he'll like that."

Chloe ran out of the room, intent on her mission.

Amy turned to Luke. "Thanks for getting here quickly."

"I was glad to help, but you had the situation under control. The compression bandage buys time, and the ambulance got here fast."

"True."

He frowned. "Do you know what happened to the snake?"

She shivered. "I think the snake was more scared of the storm than we were. I've never seen a tiger snake rear up like that one did."

"Me, either. But Declan is fine and the snake will go back to its burrow or tree stump."

"Hopefully that's a long way from the house."

"Maybe. Ben needs to make sure it's not living under the house."

"I don't want to even think about it." She dragged her teeth over her lower lip. "My clothes are in the sports bag on the backseat."

He nodded. "I'll be back soon."

She headed to Declan's bedroom, ready to pack an overnight bag. Could Ben forgive her for putting his son's life in danger?

Amy pulled into a parking spot outside Snowgum Creek Hospital. The stark brick building was quiet for a Friday afternoon. Luke had parked in his doctor's reserved space next to the main entrance and had taken Chloe inside ahead of her. Chloe had been excited by the prospect of riding in Uncle Luke's new Jeep with plush leather seats.

She greeted the receptionist and nurses in the emergency department before making her way to Declan's examination room.

Ben sat beside Declan's bed, holding his son's hand. Chloe knelt in a chair next to her father, and Luke stood at the end of the bed, reading Declan's chart.

Declan's eyes were closed and his leg remained wrapped in the bandage.

She paused inside the doorway, meeting Ben's exhausted gaze. "How's he doing?"

"Good, I think. The antivenin is doing the job."

"Yes," Luke said. "They'll keep him in overnight as a precaution, but he'll make a full recovery."

She sighed. "That's good news."

Ben's mother appeared behind her. "How is my precious grandson?"

"On the mend," Ben said. He gave his mother a brief update.

After a short visit, Ben's mom said, "Chloe, I think you

should come back to my place now and see your grandpa. I baked your favorite cookies this afternoon."

Chloe's face brightened. "White choc chip." She kissed her father's cheek. "See you later, Dad."

Ben smiled. "You be good."

"I will." Chloe left the room with her grandmother.

Luke glanced at his watch. "I'm due back at the clinic, but I'll swing by in a few hours to check on his progress."

Ben nodded. "Thanks for everything."

"No worries." Luke waved goodbye and left the room.

Amy sat in the vacant chair next to Ben. His rigid posture worried her and she placed her hand on his shoulder.

"You look worn-out. Can I get you something? Coffee, food?"

He shook his head, making no move to touch her. "I can wait. I don't want him to stir and be alone in this room. The snakebite was scary enough…."

She dropped her hand to her side and shrank back, his rejection stinging. The door opened and Rachel came into the room, her face full of concern.

"How's he doing?"

Ben looked up. "Much better."

Rachel frowned. "You look wiped out."

He slouched back in his seat. "So I've heard, but I need to stay here in case he wakes up."

Rachel placed her hands on her hips. "You need a break. I'll stay with Declan, and Amy can find you something to eat and drink."

"Thanks, Rach." He stood, looking preoccupied with his own thoughts.

Amy left the room first and waited for him to catch up. "The cafeteria may be open. Or we can hit the vending machines?"

He shrugged. "I don't care. You decide."

"Sure. We'll try the cafeteria first." She walked beside him, the emotional gulf growing between them.

She nibbled her lower lip, her guilt and insecurities rising to the surface. He must blame her for Declan's near-death experience.

"Would you like a coffee? Or something to eat?"

"Coffee will do. I'm not hungry."

He waited in silence while she ordered their coffees. They found a secluded table in a corner of the cafeteria.

She ripped open a sugar packet and stirred the granules into her latte.

He sipped his coffee, staring into the distance.

She swallowed hard. "Ben, is everything okay?"

"Yep."

"It was a shock seeing that snake." She shivered. "Luke wondered if it was living near the house."

He nodded. "I hope not, but I haven't seen any tiger snakes that close to the house."

"It's a worry. Do you see many tiger snakes?"

"No, but I'll take a look around tomorrow."

"Good idea. That hailstorm was freaky. I'd forgotten about how fast the weather can change."

"Yep, it's not fun."

She sipped her latte. "Is there much damage in the orchards?"

He tensed, drawing his brows together. "I'll find out tomorrow."

She nodded. The hail netting should have protected part of the orchard from the destructive storm.

He drained his coffee cup. "I need to get back to Declan."

She widened her eyes, his brusque tone squeezing her heart. "Is there anything I can do?"

"Not today." He pushed his chair back and stood. "I should buy Rachel a drink."

"I can do that—"

"No, I'll get it." He rubbed his hand over his face. "I'm in for a long night."

She bit her lower lip. "I might get going, then, if you don't need anything."

He frowned. "Okay. I need time to think about a few things."

She blinked away a stray tear. "Can you call me later to let me know how Declan is doing?" He was pushing her away because she'd failed him.

"Sure." He crossed his arms over his chest and stared at the floor. "See you later."

She spun on her heel and walked away, dabbing her fingertips on the outer corners of her eyes. He had forced her to face the awful truth. How could he love her after she had put his son's life in danger? Jenny would never have made such a stupid mistake. She was sure of that.

She quickened her pace, her heart ripping apart as she remembered the pain Declan had experienced after the snakebite. It was all her fault, and she didn't deserve the responsibility of a husband and children.

Chapter 16

Ben rubbed his fingers over his weary eyes and slumped in his seat beside Declan's bed. His mother had brought him a light dinner and he'd picked at the pasta, his appetite gone. Declan was now resting comfortably and was fast asleep, his rhythmic breathing the only sound in the room.

Ben glanced at his watch. Luke was due to arrive any minute. The pungent antiseptic odor in the room brought back memories of Jenny's numerous hospital visits. He'd spent hours by her bedside, helpless to stop the cancer that ravaged her body.

He let out a deep breath, relieved that Declan was responding well to the treatment.

He rolled his shoulders, releasing some of the tension in his back. He'd stay here for another hour before collecting Chloe from his parents and catching a lift home with his brother. Tomorrow morning he'd inspect the damage in the orchards and prepare for another tough year on a lean budget.

Luke appeared in the doorway. "How's everything going?"

"Good, I think."

His brother read Declan's chart. "I'm happy with his progress. But you, on the other hand, look shattered."

Ben met Luke's concerned gaze. "It hasn't been a good day."

"Close encounters with tiger snakes aren't fun." Luke frowned. "Especially knowing the snake is still on the loose."

Ben nodded. "I'll worry about the snake tomorrow." He kept the yard clear of debris that attracted snakes, but the dry summer weather sometimes brought them too close to the house for his liking.

"Okay." Luke sat in the chair beside him and stretched out his legs. "One of the nurses will bring us coffee soon."

Ben raised an eyebrow. "Which nurse, exactly?"

"Bronwyn. She's one of my friends from Sunny Ridge Hospital."

"Oh, I see."

Luke chuckled. "I don't think you do. She's older than our mother and grateful I helped her fix a problem on my way in here."

"Are you on call tonight?"

"Yes, from ten. I can drive you and Chloe home without being interrupted or held up."

Ben nodded. "I appreciate your help."

"Too easy. You know I adore the kids."

He sat up straighter in his seat. Declan hadn't stirred, his face peaceful as he slept through their conversation. "You'll make a great dad, one day."

Luke shrugged. "That's assuming I can find someone who'll put up with me and my crazy work schedule."

"I told you before that women are queuing at the door."

"Maybe, but the life of a country doctor's wife isn't easy."

Ben ran his hand over the whiskers shadowing his jaw. "According to Amy, city life isn't any better."

Luke frowned. "Where is Amy? I thought she'd be here with you tonight."

Ben stared at his feet, avoiding Luke's gaze.

"Ben, what happened? Did you two have a fight?"

"No, I…wanted to have some time to think."

"Did you tell her to go home?"

"Not exactly. I just needed some space."

Luke was quiet for a moment, seeming to gather his thoughts together. "Have you seen the orchards?"

Ben sighed. "Nope. Did you take a look?"

"I didn't have time, but there was a fair bit of ice on the ground."

"Yep. I saw too much hail on the ground to have any hope." The patches of white in the orchards were etched in his brain, a stark reminder of all he had lost.

"It may not be as bad as it looks."

He shook his head. "It's worse. To be honest, I'm dreading what I'll see in the morning."

"You can sell the apples for juice and recoup some money."

"True, but the crop was beautiful and top quality. For a change, the projected market prices are actually good this year for the high-grade produce."

"The netting should have protected some of the crop."

"But not enough to make a real difference." The hail netting had likely helped, but he couldn't afford the cost of covering the whole orchard.

Luke sat forward in his chair. "What's your hunch on the damage?"

"I don't think there'll be much to salvage from the un-covered trees. I should break even if the prices stay up, but it will mean another year of scrimping to pay the bills."

"Oh, that's why you're pushing Amy away?"

He narrowed his eyes. "Who said I'm doing that?"

"I know Amy, and I know she'd want to be here tonight with you."

"I have nothing to offer her."

Luke snorted. "That's a load of rubbish and you know it."

"Do you know the full extent of her husband's wealth? She lived in a mansion in one of the best suburbs in Sydney."

"Who cares? I know all that money didn't make for a happy marriage."

"That's not the point."

"Really?"

"I have farm debt and no cash flow. She deserves a husband who can afford to look after her."

"You do realize she has a well-paying job and probably a savings account and investments? She can look after herself and can afford to pay her way."

He grimaced. "That just makes it worse."

"How?" Luke shook his head. "If you marry Amy, she won't be a financial burden and she might even be able to help you invest in the farm. How's that a bad thing?"

"I can't use her money to pay for farm expenses."

"Why? Did you and Jenny keep separate bank accounts?"

"This is different."

"How?" Luke rubbed his fingers through his hair. "I don't understand why you're being so stubborn. Whether or not she has money shouldn't be an issue. If you love each other, and I know the kids adore her, I don't see why you can't join forces and work together as a team."

"It's not that simple. Amy doesn't know how tight things are financially."

"Ben, are you crazy? Do you really think she'd reject you because you're not rolling in money?" He shook his head. "It's time you swallowed your pride and put a ring on her finger."

Ben closed his eyes, his brother's logic fighting with

Narelle Atkins 167

his pride. Was Luke right? Could he risk his heart and ask Amy to marry him, debt and all?

He opened his eyes, meeting his brother's determined gaze. "I don't know."

Luke placed a comforting hand on his shoulder. "I'll pray you make a wise decision."

Ben nodded. *Lord, please lead me in the right direction. I love Amy and I want to give her a good life, not a life of struggle and hardship.*

The next morning, Amy wiped beads of perspiration from her brow and switched off her vacuum cleaner. By ten o'clock she had cleaned her entire cottage. She walked into the kitchen, pleased the tile floor had already dried. The weather forecast was for a hot day and possible afternoon storms. She sighed. The local apple farmers didn't need more hail.

She poured a tall glass of iced tea and added ice cubes. The lemon and lime flavors teased her senses, and she drank a big mouthful. She refilled her glass and collected her Bible before heading outside to sit on her back deck overlooking the garden.

The cushions on her chair squeaked as she stretched into a more comfortable position. Two hours of cleaning felt like a gym workout, and she was glad to get it out of the way before the day became too hot.

Cleaning was therapeutic and had temporarily taken her mind off Ben. Last night, she had dreamed that a tiger snake was coiled around her bare feet, ready to strike. She'd woken with a start, her breathing shallow and perspiration soaking her bed linens.

She shook her head, trying to rid her mind of the frightening image. The truth was unavoidable. She had let Ben down. Could she forgive herself for not taking better care of Declan?

Tiny new buds sprouted on the potted rosebush. The Christmas present from Ben usually brought a smile to her lips. She blinked, the promise of a budding relationship with Ben dimming in her mind. Self-doubt haunted her, and the baggage from her previous marriage blew open in her mind. She didn't deserve to be a mother. Her infertility was a sign that she was destined to be childless.

Tears wet her cheeks as she released her pent-up stress and anxiety. She was irresponsible and couldn't even remember to feed her neighbors' cat, let alone care for children. Doug's accusations lingered in her mind, exposing new wounds she had thought were healed. His negativity and determination to blame her for their marital woes had torn her apart, and now the memories threatened to derail the positive progress she'd made since moving home to Snowgum Creek.

She bit her lip and choked back a sob. How could Ben trust her to take care of his children after the spectacular way she had messed up yesterday? He deserved someone who was responsible and more like his beloved Jenny. She imagined Jenny had never put her children's lives in danger. The woman was close to perfect in Amy's mind. Everyone had loved Jenny and admired her strong faith.

Lord, I'm thankful Declan is fine, but I can't stop thinking about the worst-case scenario. I love Ben and the children, but I don't deserve to be a part of their family. It hurts too much to contemplate not being a part of their lives. Please give me strength to survive the inevitable breakup now that Ben realizes I'm not good enough for him.

She reached for her Bible and flipped it open to the Psalms where she had left off yesterday. King David's words in Psalm 18 were a balm for her wounded spirit. She closed her eyes for a moment, drawing on the Lord's strength. David had been a great king and was described as a man after God's heart. Yet David had made mistakes and was fallible like the rest of humanity. God didn't abandon David in his time of need.

She let out a deep breath. God's love for her was constant, despite her failings. He was her rock and savior.

Ben hadn't called her since she'd left the hospital the night before. She assumed Declan was on his way home this morning. Her phone was wedged in her pocket, and she took it out, staring at the blank screen. Her stomach tightened and she tried to douse her disappointment.

She sipped her iced tea, the tangy liquid soothing her dry throat. Her tears had subsided and she focused her mind on prayer.

Minutes later, her phone rang and she checked the caller ID. Ben. She gulped and answered the call with a hoarse greeting.

"Amy, are you free for lunch? There are a few things we need to discuss."

Her grip tightened on the phone. The moment of truth was drawing near. "Yes. Um, where do you want to meet?"

"My place, if that's okay. Chloe's at a friend's house, but I need to keep an eye on Declan."

"Okay. Do you want me to bring anything?"

"It's all good. I bought food this morning while I was in town. How does midday sound?"

"Fine." She had plenty of time to shower and get organized. And fret over the outcome of their lunch. "How's Declan doing?"

"Much better."

"I'm relieved to hear this."

"We're all glad he's feeling a lot better today. See you soon."

The line disconnected and she froze, her thoughts spiraling in a tailspin. Why did he sound upbeat and happy?

A flicker of hope resurrected in her heart and she stared

at the rosebush. The buds promised to bloom into beautiful flowers. Was it possible Ben had forgiven her and wanted a future with her?

Ben stashed his phone in his pocket and wandered through his house to the family room. Declan lay on the sofa, his eyes glued to a cartoon on the television.

"Amy's coming over for lunch."

His son nodded. "Can I go outside soon?"

"Do you feel up to it?"

"I'm bored, and there's no cricket to watch until later."

"I'm heading out into the orchards now, if you want to come with me."

Declan sat up, a bright smile covering his face. "Can I ride my bike?"

"I think you need to let your leg heal first. How does a ride with me on the four-wheeler sound?"

"Cool." Declan shoved his feet into his sneakers, grabbed his hat and limped outside to the shed, moving a little slower than his usual top speed.

Ben pulled the rim of his hat lower over his face, the late-morning sun heating his skin. Declan got into the passenger seat, and Ben switched on the engine, ready to assess the damage in the orchards.

He released the clutch and they headed toward the orchards that were covered by netting. As they approached the trees, he could see that the damage in this section wasn't nearly as bad as he had feared.

Declan smiled. "The hail netting protected the apples."

"Yes." Ben whispered a silent prayer of thanks. They rode up and down the rows, stopping a few times to inspect the fruit. The apples looked great and the netting had been a worthwhile investment. If the market prices held, he should break even.

He turned at the end of the last covered row and steered

the four-wheeler toward the open orchards. A flock of crows flew in and out of the trees. He drew in a steadying breath, preparing to see the worst of the storm damage.

He pulled into the first row and brought the vehicle to a halt, idling the engine.

Declan's mouth gaped open. "Dad, this looks bad."

He nodded. Apples were strewn on the ground, chunks of brown flesh exposed to the elements. Dimples covered the apples remaining on the trees. The ice bullets from the sky had wreaked havoc in this section of the orchard.

Declan jumped off the four-wheeler and reached for an apple on a low branch. He ran his small fingers over the bruised red skin, his lower lip trembling. "Dad, I feel sad."

"I know." Ben moved to Declan's side, placing a hand on his shoulder. "The hail wasn't kind to these apples."

"Can you sell them?"

"Maybe. I'll see what I can salvage when we start picking in a few weeks."

"Can I help pick these apples? I promise I'll be extra careful not to make the damaged skin worse."

"We'll see. I have a lot to do and think about before we start picking."

Declan wandered along the row, inspecting apples along the way.

Ben closed his eyes, the enormity of the damage registering in his tired brain.

The Bible verse he'd read this morning in the Gospel of Matthew came to mind. Jesus promised rest to those who came to Him, weary and heavy-laden with their burdens.

Lord, I can't do this on my own. I can't control the weather and the quality of the harvest. I trust You to look after my needs, to provide the resources to feed and clothe my children.

He opened his eyes and blew out a stream of air, his body relaxing as he started to let go of his worries. Luke was right. He had to trust that Amy loved him irrespective of the size of his bank balance. Together they could endure the hard years and celebrate when they were blessed with a bountiful harvest.

"Daddy, look what I found." Declan ran toward him, a wide grin covering his face.

"What is it?"

He held out a large red apple in both hands. "Take a look at this."

Ben examined the circumference of the apple, the red skin free from blemishes. "Where did you find this apple?"

"On a tree at the end of the row."

A thread of hope pulled his lips into a smile. "Are there many apples like this?"

Declan nodded and reached for his hand. "Come with me. I think the hail missed a few trees in that corner."

Thank You, Lord. He straightened his spine, optimism clawing its way into his mind. Was it possible the damage wouldn't be as enormous as he'd feared?

Chapter 17

Amy drove along the dirt track leading to Ben's farm, her stomach compressed into a hard ball. She squeezed the steering wheel with tense fingers, cramping her hands. She owed it to Ben, if he was prepared to forgive her, to share the painful truth about her marriage to Doug. Her relationship with Ben should be based on honesty, with no secrets from the past that could come between them. If he still wanted her after learning the truth, she'd know for certain that he loved her for the right reasons.

She parked in her usual spot, the dense foliage from overhanging branches sheltering her car from the harsh midday sun. Sunglasses shaded her eyes as she strolled to the back door and tried to calm her nerves. *Lord, please give me the right words to say and give Ben an understanding heart.*

Ben appeared on the doorstep, his mouth curved up in a smile. "Hey, Amy, good to see you."

She nodded, her words choking in her throat. "You, too."

He wore knee-length cargo shorts and an old T-shirt, his muscular arms stretching the sleeves tight over his bronzed skin.

She stashed her sunglasses in her purse and followed Ben inside the house. He walked ahead and made no move to touch her. Her anxiety intensified. Was he planning to break up with her?

She entered the kitchen. Sunlight filtered in through the open curtains, giving the room a cozy atmosphere.

Ben pointed to the coffeemaker. "Coffee or a cool drink?"

She lifted a brow. "You've worked out how to use it."

He nodded. "More importantly, I think I've learned how to make coffee the way you like it."

Her mouth relaxed into a smile. "Coffee sounds good." She'd spent the past month trying to teach Ben how to use the coffeemaker. Last week, he had confessed that he only used it when she visited.

Declan ran into the kitchen. "Hi, Amy."

"Hey, Declan, how are you feeling?"

He was red in the face, and his breathing was shallow, as if he'd run a long distance. "Good, and happy to be home."

She let out a sigh. "I'm glad you made a fast recovery."

"Me, too. Dad, can I have a drink?"

His father gave him a stern look. "And how do you ask for a drink?"

Declan huffed, wrinkling his nose. "Can I please have a drink of juice?"

"That's better." Ben walked over to the fridge. "I'll also fill a water bottle for you to take outside."

"Thanks, Dad."

"It's a scorcher today. Have you put on more sunscreen?"

His son pulled a face. "I hate sunscreen."

"There's colored zinc cream in the bathroom for your face." Ben frowned. "I can come in and help you—"

"No, Dad, I'll do it." Declan beamed a cheeky smile

at Amy. "I'm wearing my cricket hat today. Can we play cricket later?"

She nodded. "When the weather cools down. I'm surprised you're not melting in the sun."

"Lily is resting under the veranda steps in the shade, and I filled her water bowl to the brim."

Ben smiled and handed his son a plastic cup of juice. "I was about to go outside and refill it myself."

"Thanks, Dad." Declan gulped from the plastic cup.

"You sure are thirsty," Ben said.

Declan nodded, his attention focused on quenching his thirst.

An air-conditioning unit hummed in the background, keeping this part of the house cool and comfortable. Her sleeveless shirt and shorts had clung to her skin during the drive to the farm, despite the air-conditioning running on the coldest setting.

Declan downed the remainder of his juice, grabbed the water bottle and raced out of the kitchen.

The aroma of freshly brewed coffee tantalized her taste buds. Ben passed her a mug.

"Our lunch is in the fridge, ready to serve when you're hungry. Do you want to have your coffee inside or on the veranda?"

"Inside, if that's okay. Unless you need to be outside to watch Declan?"

He shook his head. "You wouldn't know he was only discharged from hospital this morning. That kid is an indestructible bundle of energy."

She sipped her coffee, appreciating the strong brew. "I'm impressed. The blend is smooth and strong in flavor."

He tasted a sample from his mug. "Yes, I finally got it right, and I'm glad you like it."

"It's good." She followed Ben into the family room and

settled beside him on the sofa. "I'm so glad Declan's okay, especially since it's all my fault."

His eyes widened. "I don't follow. How is the snakebite your fault?"

She ran the tip of her tongue over dry lips before drinking a sip of coffee. She stared at the mug as if it held the answers to her problems. "I forgot to make sure the laundry door was closed. I was on my way to check when I was distracted by something and then the storm hit."

"Amy." He tilted her chin up toward him with his thumb, holding her gaze. "Have you been blaming yourself for the snakebite?"

She nodded. "I'm sorry." He dropped his hand and she missed the rough texture of his calloused fingers beneath her chin.

"Hey, there's no need to apologize." He cradled his coffee mug in both hands. "I don't hold you responsible for what happened to Declan."

"Really?" Hope sprang to life in her heart.

"It was nobody's fault. Who could have predicted a tiger snake would be on the lawn? Or that Declan would run straight into its path?" He drained his mug before placing it on the coffee table. "Declan is old enough to know better than to run outside in storms. His lack of impulse control is constantly getting him into trouble."

"I'm relieved he's okay." She swallowed her last mouthful of coffee and rested the empty mug on a nearby coaster.

"Me, too." Ben rubbed his hand through his hair. "Yesterday wasn't a good day, and the orchards are a mess."

She frowned. "Did the hail netting help?"

"To a point. The apples under the netting are fine, but only a small part of the orchard has netting."

"Can you salvage any of the apples that weren't covered?"

"Maybe. But the prices for juice aren't good."

She placed her hand in his. "That explains a lot."

He held her gaze, lacing his fingers through hers. "What do you mean?"

"You've been distant since the storm."

"Yep." He cleared his throat. "I was counting on a big crop combined with great prices to get ahead financially. A few of the varieties will be ready to pick in a couple of weeks."

If only the hail had held off until the picking was done. She sighed. His misery was etched on his face. "There's always next year."

"Yes, I've been saying that every year for three years." He grimaced. "Life on the land is hard. The weather is unreliable and you can lose your crop in a matter of minutes."

Amy nodded. "It sounds like you're due for a good year soon."

"I hope so, and every year I pray for a good harvest."

"Another prayer that isn't always answered the way you want or hope."

He looked deeply into her eyes. "I guess what I'm asking is—do you want this type of life? Full of uncertainty and dependent on the whims of the weather?"

She sucked in a deep breath. "Before I answer, there's something I need to tell you. It may change your mind about even asking me that question."

He furrowed his brow. "What's wrong?"

She tightened her grip on his hand, comforted by his strength. "You've been honest about your marriage to Jenny and your struggle to accept that she's gone."

He nodded. "I'm not sure I follow you."

"My marriage to Doug was very different. We had a number of issues and didn't agree on a lot of things."

"That's normal. Jenny and I had our ups and downs."

She nibbled her lower lip. "It wasn't just ups and downs.

Our marriage was fractured and broken, especially toward the end."

His eyes softened. "Oh, Amy, I'm sorry you lost Doug before you could make things right."

"He died in the Maldives. A diving accident." Her tone came out flat.

"That's awful. How devastating to lose him with no warning or time to prepare. I'm sure you're not keen to return to the Maldives."

She blinked, moisture building in her eyes. "I was in Sydney when it happened."

His eyebrows shot up. "You weren't with him?"

She shook her head, her lips trembling. "He went on a diving holiday with friends. Our last conversation wasn't pleasant."

"What happened?" Concern radiated in his voice, and he moved closer, his leg resting next to hers.

She swiped the back of her hand across her eyes, catching a few rogue tears before meeting his gentle gaze. "He told me our marriage was over and he wanted me to move out before he returned home."

Ben drew Amy into his arms. "I'm so sorry."

She sniffed, her face buried against his chest. "I did everything I could to please him."

"I'm sure you did." Doug sounded like an idiot. Ben remembered hearing about the fiasco at Bella's wedding a few years back, when Doug had snubbed Amy's family by being aloof. The whole town had thought Doug's behavior was arrogant and rude.

"I was a failure as a wife the first time around."

He grunted and stroked her hair. "It does take two, you know. It sounds like he wasn't a particularly good husband. Did you go to counseling?"

"Doug refused. He couldn't accept my infertility."

"Did you look into adoption?"

"No, Doug was worried that people might think *he* was infertile." She paused, her body rigid in his arms. "He really didn't want a child for the right reasons."

"Now I'm confused. He was prepared to leave you because you couldn't provide him with a child that he didn't really want?"

She looked up, her eyes glassy. "It was all about money. He inherited an extra million from his grandmother for every child he sired, to be held in a family trust."

He felt his jaw drop. "Wow. That's a lot of money."

"And a lot of pressure. His grandmother was in her seventies and Doug blamed me for ruining his opportunity to increase the size of his inheritance."

"I'm so sorry you had to live through such an awful experience." How could Doug value money more than his marriage to Amy?

She let out a big breath. "Now you know the horrible truth. You're the only person, other than a grief counselor I saw in Sydney, who knows how bad things were at the end. I begged Doug to give us another chance, to work together to find a solution."

"But he wouldn't listen."

"He had made up his mind that he was leaving. Five days later I received a phone call from the authorities advising me of his death. I'd seen a news report on an Aussie death in the Maldives but never dreamed it was my husband."

"You poor thing." He cupped her damp cheek in his hand. "It must have been a big shock."

She nodded, tears running down her cheeks. "Since we parted on bad terms, I wasn't expecting to hear from him, and the phone call about his death was a nightmare. His parents never liked me and they already knew about Doug's plan to leave me. Doug had updated his will before he left, and I ended up with the small settlement he'd planned to offer me when he returned."

He drew her closer, rubbing his hand over the small of her back. "You are worth much more than a million dollars."

She blinked, her tears starting to subside. "You think so?"

He nodded. "Doug was crazy to even contemplate leaving you. I may not have much money, but I know your worth is infinitely greater than his potential inheritance."

"I don't care about money. I have enough to live a comfortable life in Snowgum Creek. Whether or not you have money doesn't matter to me."

His heart warmed at her earnest tone and kind words. "I'm glad to hear this."

He dipped his head and brushed his lips over hers. God had answered his prayers today.

Amy swallowed her last mouthful of salad, her stomach replete. Ben had arranged for his parents to babysit the children and he'd cooked a romantic dinner for two. She sat beside him at the large dining-room table, a candle burning on an antique silver candlestick in front of them. A fragrant bouquet of pink and mauve roses was displayed in a large crystal vase.

She smiled. "I noticed the baked cheesecake in the fridge."

"Yes, it looks good."

"I think I need a break before dessert. I'm full already."

He grinned. "We are changing location for dessert."

"Really." She leaned her elbow on the table, her hand under her chin. "I'm intrigued by your plans."

"I promise you'll like them." He stood and held out his hand.

She placed her hand in his and rose from her chair. "The gazebo?"

"No, but you're getting closer."

She wrinkled her brow, glancing down at her fitted pink summer dress and strappy sandals. "Do I need to change my clothes or shoes?"

He laughed. "I'll carry you if we see a snake."

She playfully slapped his arm. "That's not funny."

"We'll be walking a short distance, but the ground is even."

"Be prepared for me to leap into your arms."

He winked. "That won't be a hardship." He led her out of the dining room and along the hall to the kitchen.

"Can I help with anything?"

"Yes. Can you please fill the thermos with coffee?"

"Sure." She found the thermos on the kitchen counter and started making coffee the way she liked it, her hands on autopilot. Ben had made a big effort tonight to impress her with dinner. He'd taken the children trout fishing early this morning in the mountains to catch fresh fish for tonight's meal.

He removed a small picnic basket from a kitchen cupboard. "Would you like whipped cream or ice cream with your cheesecake?"

"Whipped cream is fine." Sunset was half an hour away, and ice cream might melt in the summer-evening heat.

"Okay." He placed the cheesecake on the counter and sliced two generous servings.

"It looks delicious."

"I hope so." He pulled containers of whipped cream and sliced fruit out of the fridge. "I used a few lemons from the tree. They're usually quite sweet." He put the dessert in deep bowls and covered them in plastic wrap.

She filled the thermos with coffee. "I'm all done."

"Great." He held the picnic basket and reached for her hand. "Let's go."

She walked beside Ben through the orchards she'd grown

to love, the aroma of fresh coffee lingering around the thermos she carried. They climbed up the gentle hill overlooking the western orchards to the highest ridge on the property.

She reached the summit and gasped. "Ben, this is beautiful."

A small table with two chairs was set up to take advantage of the imminent sunset.

He pulled her close to his side, dropping a kiss on her cheek. "I remembered how much you like this spot in the orchard." He removed a heavy cloth he had used as a table covering, revealing cutlery and coffee mugs laid out on crisp white linen.

"Wow. When did you have time to set this up?"

He grinned. "I have my ways."

"Oh, I remember now." He had ducked away just before he started panfrying the trout. Their time together today had been full of revelations. She had learned the secret combination of ingredients in his salad dressing while they chatted in the kitchen.

He pulled out a chair and she sat down, her gaze taking in the beauty of the rolling hills. Hues of pink and orange streaked the sky, providing a reflective glow on the puffy white clouds gathering on the horizon.

He unwrapped their bowls and placed them on the table. "Coffee now or later?"

"I should wait, but it smells so good."

"I agree." He poured two cups of coffee and sat beside her.

The sky continued to change, the kaleidoscope of colors providing a gorgeous backdrop for dessert. She sampled the cheesecake, the smooth texture gliding down her throat.

"Ben, this is good. You were right about the lemons."

He nodded. "They make a nice lemon butter, too." He held her hand, twining his fingers with hers. "I wanted tonight to be perfect."

"I think you succeeded."

"Not yet." He stood and walked around the table, pausing when he was right in front of her. He grabbed a small jewelry box from his pocket and dropped down on one knee.

Her mouth opened, but no words came out. Her heart raced and she drew in a steadying breath.

He gently held her left hand, as if it was more precious than gold. "Amy, I love you and I can't imagine my life without you." His warm brown eyes held her gaze. "Will you do me the great honor of becoming my wife?"

She nodded, her heart bursting with joy. "Yes. I love you and the children so much."

He popped open the jewelry box. A vintage art-deco diamond solitaire ring sparkled in the golden light filling the orchard.

She gasped. "Ben, I love it."

"I hope it fits. I ran out of time to check the sizing." He slid the ring onto her finger, the band a little bit loose as it settled below her knuckle.

"One size too big. An easy fix."

He cupped her cheek, drawing her face toward him. His lips met hers and she leaned closer, welcoming his kiss. He ran his hand through her hair, twisting a lock around his fingers.

Her pulse raced and she caressed his muscular neck and shoulders, her body alive with the knowledge that they belonged together.

He drew back, his breathing ragged. "We have plans to make, a wedding date to set. I don't want a long engagement."

"Me, either, but we need to consider the children. They may need time to adjust."

He shook his head. "Chloe and Declan have already asked when we're getting married, and they've given us their blessing."

A stray tear fell from the corner of her eye. "They are darling children."

"And I couldn't be happier." He stood and drew her to her feet. "Look at the sunset."

The sky was alive with brilliant shades of pink, her favorite color. She snuggled in the circle of his arms, her head resting under his chin. "Thank you. I couldn't have asked for a more romantic marriage proposal."

He dropped a kiss on the top of her head. "How does March sound? Hopefully your father can fit us into his church wedding schedule."

"Sounds wonderful. I don't want a big fuss."

"We could hire caterers and have a small reception here. Our families could pitch in and help."

"A great idea. A March wedding would be perfect." Her heart swelled as they started making wedding plans. Her prayers had been answered and she'd soon have a family of her own to love and cherish.

Chapter 18

Amy stood inside the main entrance of Snowgum Creek Community Church, her hand tucked into the crook of her father's arm. She clasped her bouquet of roses, nervous twinges flittering in her stomach.

Rachel adjusted Amy's veil, the gauzy fabric settling on her bare shoulders. "Amy, you look stunning."

"Thanks." Amy drew in a calming breath, remembering how her sleek ivory-silk gown highlighted her fair complexion. Her blond locks were pinned up and held in place by a diamond-encrusted antique gold hair comb. "And you look fabulous in pink."

Rachel nodded, her attention now focused on the children. Chloe held Declan's hand, her long pink dress matching her bouquet of flowers. Declan looked like a smaller version of his handsome daddy in his suit and bow tie.

The music changed and Rachel smiled. "It's time." She stepped between her niece and nephew, taking hold of their hands as they headed up the aisle.

Her father leaned in closer and whispered in her ear. "Are you ready?"

She nodded. "Let's do it." She stepped forward with her father, acknowledging the beaming smiles of the guests in the back rows. There was only one smile she wanted to see.

Ben stood tall beside Luke, his unruly dark hair trimmed since she'd seen him yesterday afternoon. His brown eyes widened and she held his smoldering gaze, each step taking her closer to the man she loved.

At last, she stood beside Ben, and he lowered his head, his voice soft. "You look incredible."

Her pulse raced. "So do you."

Her father's dear friend, who had also been Ben's pastor in Sunny Ridge, commenced the ceremony. She threaded her fingers through Ben's, his warm grasp reassuring. Chloe and Declan stood to the side with Luke and Rachel, their small faces revealing their happiness. A rush of maternal love filled her heart. Today she would become their stepmother.

The ceremony passed in a blur. Her father took over officiating the ceremony after he completed his father-of-the-bride duties. He gave a short talk and before long she was facing Ben, repeating her wedding vows.

The depth of love shining out of Ben's eyes stole her breath. His genuine commitment to love, honor and cherish her for the rest of their lives was a blessing from God Himself. Never in her wildest dreams had she imagined she'd meet a man like Ben. A man of integrity who shared her values and beliefs. A man who was prepared to make sacrifices for her because he loved her with his whole heart.

She sent up a prayer of thanks to her heavenly father. No longer was her infertility a problem or obstacle in her life. Chloe and Declan were a precious gift and she promised to love and care for them.

Her father cleared his throat, his eyes misty. "Friends,

I present to you Mr. and Mrs. Morton. Ben, you may now kiss your bride."

Ben stepped toward her, his gaze intense. "The moment I've been waiting for," he whispered. His hands spanned her waist and he dipped his head.

She closed her eyes, his soft lips exploring the contours of her mouth. She parted her lips and he deepened the kiss. Loud applause erupted from the congregation.

He drew back and held her gaze, his eyes twinkling.

She caught her breath, her mind spinning from his irresistible kiss. They followed Luke and Rachel to a small table. She sat in a plush red-velvet seat and signed her name on the marriage certificate, smiling for photographs with Ben close by her side.

The formalities over, she held Ben's hand and walked back down the aisle. Her wide smile was firmly in place as she greeted well-wishers and accepted their congratulations. Luke and Rachel followed closely behind with the children. They stood together on the church steps, the afternoon sun highlighting the golden hues in the fallen leaves gathering on the ground.

Chloe moved to her side and gave her a bone-crunching hug. "I love you, Amy."

Her heart melted. "I love you, too, sweetheart."

"I never stopped believing and praying you'd marry my daddy."

She kissed Chloe's cheek. "God has blessed us all today." She turned to Ben, his loving gaze lingering on her face.

His smile broadened. "Who would've thought I'd rescue my future wife on a dark and isolated country road?"

She cupped his cheek in her hand. "I'm no longer abandoned and alone."

"No, you belong with us forever."

She snuggled closer to Ben, his protective arm draped around her shoulders. They had planned an afternoon reception at the farm before the children left with Ben's parents. They would spend their first night as a married couple together on the farm. Ben refused to disclose their coastal honeymoon destination, his only clue being a suggestion to pack clothes suitable for the beach.

The children stood in front of them as cameras flashed. A crowd had gathered on the circular drive after their guests had exited from the side door. Her heart overflowed with love for her new family, and an overwhelming peace filled her soul. *Lord, thank You for blessing me with an amazing family who are my perfect match.*

* * * * *

REQUEST YOUR FREE BOOKS!

2 FREE INSPIRATIONAL NOVELS
PLUS 2 FREE MYSTERY GIFTS

Love Inspired

YES! Please send me 2 FREE Love Inspired® novels and my 2 FREE mystery gifts (gifts are worth about $10). After receiving them, if I don't wish to receive any more books, I can return the shipping statement marked "cancel." If I don't cancel, I will receive 6 brand-new novels every month and be billed just $4.74 per book in the U.S. or $5.24 per book in Canada. That's a savings of at least 21% off the cover price. It's quite a bargain! Shipping and handling is just 50¢ per book in the U.S. and 75¢ per book in Canada.* I understand that accepting the 2 free books and gifts places me under no obligation to buy anything. I can always return a shipment and cancel at any time. Even if I never buy another book, the two free books and gifts are mine to keep forever.

105/305 IDN F49N

Name	(PLEASE PRINT)	
Address		Apt. #
City	State/Prov.	Zip/Postal Code

Signature (if under 18, a parent or guardian must sign)

Mail to the Harlequin® Reader Service:
IN U.S.A.: P.O. Box 1867, Buffalo, NY 14240-1867
IN CANADA: P.O. Box 609, Fort Erie, Ontario L2A 5X3

**Are you a subscriber to Love Inspired books
and want to receive the larger-print edition?
Call 1-800-873-8635 or visit www.ReaderService.com.**

* Terms and prices subject to change without notice. Prices do not include applicable taxes. Sales tax applicable in N.Y. Canadian residents will be charged applicable taxes. Offer not valid in Quebec. This offer is limited to one order per household. Not valid for current subscribers to Love Inspired books. All orders subject to credit approval. Credit or debit balances in a customer's account(s) may be offset by any other outstanding balance owed by or to the customer. Please allow 4 to 6 weeks for delivery. Offer available while quantities last.

Your Privacy—The Harlequin® Reader Service is committed to protecting your privacy. Our Privacy Policy is available online at www.ReaderService.com or upon request from the Harlequin Reader Service.
We make a portion of our mailing list available to reputable third parties that offer products we believe may interest you. If you prefer that we not exchange your name with third parties, or if you wish to clarify or modify your communication preferences, please visit us at www.ReaderService.com/consumerschoice or write to us at Harlequin Reader Service Preference Service, P.O. Box 9062, Buffalo, NY 14269. Include your complete name and address.

LIDIR13R

REQUEST YOUR FREE BOOKS!

2 FREE INSPIRATIONAL NOVELS
PLUS 2
FREE
MYSTERY GIFTS

Love Inspired
HISTORICAL
INSPIRATIONAL HISTORICAL ROMANCE

YES! Please send me 2 FREE Love Inspired® Historical novels and my 2 FREE mystery gifts (gifts are worth about $10). After receiving them, if I don't wish to receive any more books, I can return the shipping statement marked "cancel." If I don't cancel, I will receive 4 brand-new novels every month and be billed just $4.74 per book in the U.S. or $5.24 per book in Canada. That's a savings of at least 21% off the cover price. It's quite a bargain! Shipping and handling is just 50¢ per book in the U.S. and 75¢ per book in Canada.* I understand that accepting the 2 free books and gifts places me under no obligation to buy anything. I can always return a shipment and cancel at any time. Even if I never buy another book, the two free books and gifts are mine to keep forever.

102/302 IDN F5CY

Name	(PLEASE PRINT)	
Address		Apt. #
City	State/Prov.	Zip/Postal Code

Signature (if under 18, a parent or guardian must sign)

Mail to the Harlequin® Reader Service:
IN U.S.A.: P.O. Box 1867, Buffalo, NY 14240-1867
IN CANADA: P.O. Box 609, Fort Erie, Ontario L2A 5X3

Want to try two free books from another series?
Call 1-800-873-8635 or visit www.ReaderService.com.

* Terms and prices subject to change without notice. Prices do not include applicable taxes. Sales tax applicable in N.Y. Canadian residents will be charged applicable taxes. Offer not valid in Quebec. This offer is limited to one order per household. Not valid for current subscribers to Love Inspired Historical books. All orders subject to credit approval. Credit or debit balances in a customer's account(s) may be offset by any other outstanding balance owed by or to the customer. Please allow 4 to 6 weeks for delivery. Offer available while quantities last.

Your Privacy—The Harlequin® Reader Service is committed to protecting your privacy. Our Privacy Policy is available online at www.ReaderService.com or upon request from the Harlequin Reader Service.

We make a portion of our mailing list available to reputable third parties that offer products we believe may interest you. If you prefer that we not exchange your name with third parties, or if you wish to clarify or modify your communication preferences, please visit us at www.ReaderService.com/consumerschoice or write to us at Harlequin Reader Service Preference Service, P.O. Box 9062, Buffalo, NY 14269. Include your complete name and address.

LIHDIR13R

ReaderService.com

Manage your account online!

- Review your order history
- Manage your payments
- Update your address

**We've designed
the Harlequin® Reader Service
website just for you.**

Enjoy all the features!

- Reader excerpts from any series
- Respond to mailings and special monthly offers
- Discover new series available to you
- Browse the Bonus Bucks catalog
- Share your feedback

Visit us at:

ReaderService.com